CONTENTS

CHAPTER ONE	2
CHAPTER TWO	9
CHAPTER THREE	14
CHAPTER FOUR	16
CHAPTER FIVE	23
CHAPTER SIX	28
CHAPTER SEVEN	35
CHAPTER EIGHT	37
CHAPTER NINE	44
CHAPTER TEN	48
CHAPTER ELEVEN	53
CHAPTER TWELVE	60
CHAPTER THIRTEEN	62
CHAPTER FOURTEEN	68
CHAPTER FIFTEEN	76
CHAPTER SIXTEEN	79
CHAPTER SEVENTEEN	81
CHAPTER EIGHTEEN	87
CHAPTER NINETEEN	90
CHAPTER TWENTY	92
CHAPTER TWENTY-ONE	95

CHAPTER TWENTY-TWO	100
CHAPTER TWENTY-TWO	106
CHAPTER TWENTY-THREE	109
CHAPTER TWENTY-FOUR	117
CHAPTER TWENTY-FIVE	119
CHAPTER TWENTY-SIX	124
CHAPTER TWENTY-SEVEN	128
CHAPTER TWENTY-EIGHT	133
CHAPTER TWENTY-NINE	140
CHAPTER THIRTY	144
CHAPTER THIRTY-ONE	149
CHAPTER THIRTY-TWO	152
CHAPTER THIRTY-THREE	159
CHAPTER THIRTY-FOUR	167
CHAPTER THIRTY-FIVE	171
CHAPTER THIRTY-SIX	177
CHAPTER THIRTY-SEVEN	179
CHAPTER THIRTY-EIGHT	181
CHAPTER THIRTY-NINE	184
CHAPTER FORTY	191
CHAPTER FORTY-ONE	198
CHAPTER FORTY-TWO	201
CHAPTER FORTY-THREE	202
CHAPTER FORTY-FOUR	206
CHAPTER FORTY-FIVE	209
CHAPTER FORTY-SIX	212
CHAPTER FORTY-SEVEN	215
CHAPTER FORTY-EIGHT	220

CHAPTER FORTY-NINE	223
Books In This Series	226
Books In This Series	228
Books By This Author	230

A MOTHER'S RUIN

A DI Fiona Williams Mystery

Proofreading provided by the Hyper-Speller at https://www.wordrefiner.com
COVER IMAGE - BIGSTOCK
COVER DESIGN – Diana J Febry

CHAPTER ONE

Emily Clifton stared out of her kitchen window, jaded and hollow, with her phone pressed to her ear. Her empty suitcase was by her feet while the washing machine thundered and rattled through its final spin. Through the window, the sleeves of her favourite shirt waved at her from the washing line as white clouds raced across the sky. A reminder of a life so mundane, so superficially conventional and domesticated, it hurt.

She hated making decisions. Especially one that would change everything and be irreversible. Why did adulthood have to be so difficult? Both options were crammed with snares and complications. Both destined her to sacrifice something, or someone. Where was the easy, no-brainer option where no one was hurt?

Maybe she would be different. Everything could be explained away. A lover's tiff. A childish act of revenge in the heat of the moment. Forgiven and overcome with time. It had worked before. Why not again?

Realising the phone was silent, Emily gave a heavy sigh. "It's only been a few hours, and already I miss you so much. I know you think a fresh start where nobody knows us is the only way, but there's always a chance it won't come to that. We will know soon. I'm not giving up hope until then. Melanie won't give up without a fight. She will do everything in her power to put a spanner in the works. She would kill to hold on to Katie."

Emily closed her eyes, listening to all the reasons why she had to face reality. Couldn't she dream of an easier alternative for a few weeks longer? She chewed her lip at the lie she told. She had re-written her resignation letter a hundred times in her head, so it was more of a half-lie. She just hadn't committed her thoughts to paper.

Outside grew dark without warning and huge drops of rains peppered the windowpane. "Sorry. I'm going to have to go. It has started to rain, and my washing is out. I'll call you back later. Love you."

She turned her back against the rain, straining to hear the last comment as raindrops joined up to stream down the window. The downpour would probably only last a few minutes, and the sun would reappear as though it had never been away. The washing machine whirred dramatically, reminding her she had another load to dry and put away before bedtime. Covering her ear to block out the crescendo of the final spin, she said, "Sorry, Katie hasn't been dropped off yet. She should be here in an hour or so. We will ring you later. Promise."

Over the disappointment, Emily heard something else. Something that unnerved her. They shared everything, the good and the ugly. It was the first time she sensed something was being hidden from her. "Are you okay? Is something bothering you?"

The reassuring reply sounded false. Maybe it was distortion on the line, or she imagined it? Either way, there was nothing she could do. It would have to wait until next week. "Love you. Speak later."

Emily grabbed the wash basket and ran outside. She raced against the black clouds yanking her nearly dry clothes from the line. As the intensity of the rain increased, it dampened the dusty ground, releasing a fresh smell of rebirth and new beginnings.

Woken by the sound of the shower, DI Fiona Williams rolled over to the other side of the bed. It was still warm and smelt of Stefan. He had reappeared last night after disappearing for over a month without explanation. In his absence, she had told herself repeatedly it was best he never returned. Their relationship, if she could call it that, was destined to fail. Far easier, he rode off into the sunset and never looked back.

While he had been away, she had filled her empty time going over cases where Ian Dewhurst was registered as the senior investigating officer. It had become her substitute, guilty pleasure. It probably wasn't a healthy obsession but searching for a black mark against him had distracted her from feeling sorry for herself.

He gave her the creeps, and she always made sure she was never alone in a closed room with him. He stank of sleaze and corruption although none of it had halted his rise up the police hierarchy's slippery pole. He made everyone's life miserable as he used their station as a steppingstone to greater things. She dreamed about wiping the smug, arrogant look from his face.

One case looked promising. A young woman had been strangled and her body hastily hidden in woodland. Eliot McCall had been an early suspect for good reason, yet he had been quickly dismissed from the investigation after one friendly interview.

Eliot was the son of a Tory cabinet minister. Even luckier for him, his father was Dewhurst's golfing partner. A minor detail he had failed to mention when registering himself as the SIO. Eliot's innocence had been reinforced by the headmaster of his expensive private school, describing him as a remarkable young man and a gifted student with a bright future ahead of him. It would be a terrible shame to wrongly taint such an upstanding citizen. Bla bla bla. Instead, on flimsy, mostly circumstantial evidence, a teenager from the local council state had been found guilty and was still doing time.

It wasn't only the unfairness that concerned her. A young woman had been strangled and left in woodland on the outskirts of Plymouth a few weeks ago. Her body was found near the house daddy had bought for Eliot while he studied marine biology at the university. The victim was an illegal immigrant working in a nail bar, and the investigation appeared to be buried under a mountain of more pressing concerns.

Ben Creasy claimed to have seen Eliot on the evening of the first strangulation. He had been side-lined from the investigation after Eliot's mother said he was at home studying for his exams that evening. Once Fiona had spoken to Creasy, she would have an excuse to suggest Plymouth look at Eliot McCall and the previous murder investigation overseen by Dewhurst.

She could do nothing more until Creasy contacted her, so she told herself to stop feeling guilty. It was the weekend, after all. She could be like a normal person, forget about work for a few days and enjoy her time with Stefan. While she waited for him to finish in the shower, she could daydream about them having a rosy future. She could concoct a fantasy future where she lived with Stefan as a respectable, local dentist in a rose-covered cottage. Forget about murder, corruption and facing the truth, even if it was only for a few hours.

The shrill sound of her mobile phone came from the bedside cabinet. She groaned as she rolled over to answer it. At this time of the morning, it could be one of two people. Her mother with a domestic crisis or DCI Peter Hatherall.

Fiona was scrabbling to get dressed when Stefan re-entered the room with only a small towel wrapped around his waist.

"What is this panic?" Stefan asked. "I haven't created a fire in the kitchen, cooking breakfast."

Pulling a sweater over her head, Fiona said, "I'll have to take a rain check on that. Peter is picking me up from outside in fifteen minutes."

Looking crestfallen, Stefan said, "But this is not possible, Fiona. It is weekend. I have made plans for us."

Rummaging through the bottom of her wardrobe, looking for her boots, Fiona replied, "Unfortunately, my job doesn't work like that. A woman has been found dead this morning." Pulling out a pair of walking books, she added, "If you could arrange for criminals to take the weekends off, that would be great."

Stefan walked to the bedroom window and pulled back the curtains to look outside. "Peter rings. And now, you go running."

Irritably, Fiona replied, "Yes. Peter, my boss." She sat on the bed to lace her boots, silently seething at the hint of jealousy in Stefan's tone. What right did he have to question her when she had no idea where he had been the last few weeks? They weren't even in a proper relationship. On the rare occasion they went out, they drove miles to avoid being seen together. Okay, that suited her just as much, but that wasn't the point. Looking up, she asked, "Where did you park your car?"

"It is out on the street. A few houses away." Turning to face Fiona, he asked, "Who is this woman? Is she young, old? English?"

Fiona laced her second boot and stood. "It's unlikely to be anything related to your sister, okay. The woman was found by her mother this morning. That's all I know."

"I'm sorry. That was not what I was asking. I am disappointed we won't be spending the day together, but I'm showing interest in your work."

"Yeah, right," Fiona replied, unconvinced, walking to the door. "I've enough time for a quick coffee and some toast. I've no idea what time I will be back."

Stefan followed her to the kitchen. He sat at the table while Fiona pulled out two mugs from the cupboard and shoved two pieces of bread in the toaster. She wrenched open the fridge door to take out a pint of milk before slamming it shut.

"Are you not a morning person, today?"

Keeping her back to Stefan, Fiona spooned instant coffee into the two mugs. She took a deep breath and counted silently to ten. She didn't know if she was irritated by Stefan's earlier tone or because she would be dealing with a family's worst nightmare rather than spending a morning in bed with him. Her toast popped up, and she asked, "Do you want me to put some in for you?"

"No. A coffee will be good."

When Fiona carried over the coffee and toast and sat down, Stefan said, "I am very selfish. I should think about the poor woman and her family. And poor you having to deal with it all." Cupping his hands around his mug of coffee, he added, "I will cook perfect meal for us, tonight. Very romantic. Lots of candles."

Fiona bit into her toast. It was hard to be cross with Stefan for long. Putting down her toast, she said, "I don't know how long I'm going to be. I may be home late." She found Stefan's childlike, expectant eyes impossible to resist. "I will telephone to let you know. Don't start anything until I do."

Outside, they heard a car engine followed by two sharp beeps of the horn. Fiona stood, took a quick slurp of her coffee, and headed to the front door carrying the second piece of toast. "See you later."

Closing the house door, Fiona's phone rang. Not the best of timings, but it was the witness she had been waiting to hear from. Luckily, Ben Creasy wasn't in the mood for small talk. He said he would meet her the following night in the Boars Head at Aust and hung up. She opened the car door, still thinking about the call, as she settled in the passenger seat of Peter's Audi. She glanced along the street at Stefan's car before quickly looking away to adjust her seatbelt.

Peter handed her a flask of coffee. "I thought you might need this."

If Peter had recognised Stefan's car as he drove in, he didn't say. Gratefully pouring herself a cup as he reversed out of her driveway, Fiona asked, "How come you've been allowed out from behind your desk? I thought Dewhurst had you firmly chained there."

"It seems that way, and it is driving me nuts. I wasn't designed to push paper around a desk. As I was the DCI on-call overnight, I'm damned if I'm going to give up being actively involved on this case." Indicating onto the main road, Peter added, "The sooner Dewhurst slithers further up the promotion ladder, the happier I'll be."

"There's no guarantee he will continue upwards. He could go sidewards or even down."

"You sound suspiciously over-confident. What have you heard?"

"You know the Eliot McCall case I was telling you about? The witness has agreed to see me tomorrow evening. After I've spoken to him, I will have enough to suggest Plymouth station should relook at the old case. Imagine their surprise when they discover a young man living within one mile of their murder site was discounted from a previous murder investigation because his father was such good friends with our eminent superintendent."

"And the son of a Tory bigwig, don't forget. We don't know for sure there was a strong case against him. I hope you're being careful."

"Of course." It was great that Peter cared, but she wasn't stupid. She knew she had to tread carefully and create a reason why a closed case from outside their area had appeared on her radar.

"Will you let me tip off Plymouth station as to the possible connection?"

"So, you can take all the glory?"

"No, so I can take the fallout," Peter said, glancing across at Fiona. "My career stalled years ago. Yours has just begun. Have you seen the promotion records of the two detectives who pulled Eliot McCall in for questioning?"

"No."

"Let's just say they decided to pursue careers in other fields. The fact there wasn't even a whisper in the media speaks volumes. So, you'll let me do the honours?"

"I'll see. What have we got here anyway?" Fiona asked, keen to change the subject. If Peter discovered she was meeting the witness in one of the roughest pubs in Birstall, he would want to tag along. It also crossed her mind that if Peter was recalled to his office duties, responsibility for this new case would probably pass to her.

"Emily Clifton, a twenty-eight-year-old woman found face down in her garden this morning by her mother. Multiple stab wounds and her washing line wrapped around her neck," Peter said. "The assumption is that she was attacked when collecting her washing in between yesterday afternoon and early evening, and she has been there all night."

CHAPTER TWO

Driving through Brierley, they passed a small, modern housing estate built recently by Stefan's Uncle's company, Highfield Homes. They were well-designed, up-market houses carefully arranged around a small green complete with duck pond and benches. But they looked out of place in a village of Cotswold stone cottages dating back centuries. Fiona looked away, not wanting to think too hard about how Darius Albu had obtained planning permission. She reminded herself Darius had completed his time in prison, and the greasy hands of local, outwardly respectable councillors had played their part. And Stefan wasn't Darius.

"Do you see anything of Stefan, these days?"

Peter's question sounded innocent enough, but Fiona wondered if he had recognised Stefan's car parked near her house. She racked her brain, trying to remember when Stefan bought the silver Jaguar. Was it before or after the trial of Robert Murray? Lying didn't come naturally to her, especially to Peter who knew her far too well. "Not recently," she replied, looking out the front windscreen. "How much further to the victim's house?"

Peter slowed the car as they approached the Lamb Inn and switched on the right indicator. "Not far." Turning into the single-track lane, he added, "It's down here, somewhere."

The narrow lane was lined by terraced cottages. The road dipped and ran over a small, stone bridge, and the cottages became grander and separated by extensive gardens or fields. As they rounded the first bend, a collection of police cars and vans came into sight. "Looks like we're the last to arrive," Peter said, pulling tight into the side of the road on the grass verge behind the other vehicles.

A young PC with sleepy eyes standing on guard in the front driveway took their details. Walking along the gravelled drive, Peter leaned over and quietly said to Fiona, "Ah. Do you remember the days of starting your shift straight from a night out?"

Fiona gave a vague, conspiratorial grin in response. She had never been a party animal. Even at school, she was known as a boring, goody-two-shoes with her nose always stuck in a book. Her adult, social life hadn't become any more exciting.

She was pleased to see the familiar face of PC Rachel Mann, an attractive, curvaceous blonde, walking to greet them. Over the years, their once frosty relationship had thawed. Partly because Fiona had grown less naïve and prudish, and partly because Rachel had moved on from being the station flirt to fully embracing the domestic bliss of marriage and parenthood. Leading the way along a stone pathway to the side of the cottage, Rachel said, "David Gibson arrived about ten minutes ago and is still completing his initial examination. It's not a pretty sight."

"The body or David?" Peter asked.

Laughing, Rachel said, "Take your pick."

Noticing the white-clad SOCO team moving around inside the house through the kitchen window, Fiona asked, "Have they found anything to suggest whether it's a domestic incident or a burglary gone wrong?"

"I've only seen downstairs, but it's an odd one," Rachel replied. "Personal items throughout the house have been trashed. Framed photographs smashed against walls, and mattresses pulled off beds and slashed open. That sort of thing. They've been through every room, yet money and credit cards in an open handbag have been left untouched on the kitchen table."

"Sounds like a domestic," Peter said, before thanking the young officer who handed over their romper suits and shoe covers.

While Peter and Fiona pulled on the protective suits, Rachel said, "A knife was found a small distance from the body. It looks like a standard kitchen knife available in most supermarkets. It doesn't match the set of knives found in the kitchen, but it could have been bought as a spare."

David Gibson knelt on the ground next to the body. Rachel stood to the side by the photographer, waiting for instructions. David's large frame blocked her view, so all Fiona could see was her jeans-clad legs. The woman's slip-on shoes had fallen off, revealing bare feet with carefully painted toes. A small butterfly was tattooed on her left ankle. To her right was a wash basket, half-filled with a jumble of clothes.

The washing line had been cut, leaving the remaining items dangling on the ground. She noticed the splatter of mud on a white shirt dangling at half-mast and recalled although yesterday had been a sunny and blustery day, there had been two sudden rainstorms. One at about three in the afternoon and another one early in the evening. The unfolded clothes suggested she had dashed out to collect the washing during one of those downpours.

"What's it looking like?" Peter asked, walking around David to get a better view of the body.

"She's been dead for at least twelve hours. Everything indicates this is where she was killed. Photographs have been taken. Can I roll her onto her side to get a better look?"

Turning to Rachel, Peter asked, "Do we know if the mother moved her in any way?"

Rachel stepped forwards. "She knelt by her side and touched her shoulder. Once she saw the blood and realised she was dead, she jumped back."

Peter gave the go-ahead, and David gently rolled the body to one side to peer underneath. Letting the body return to its original position, he said, "A frenzied, erratic stabbing. More of a general slashing, really. As you can see, there are a lot of defensive wounds on her arms. The strangulation was probably post-mortem. I will be able to tell you more later."

Rachel stepped forward to say, "Abbie has taken the victim's mother and her little girl back to her house, which is a short distance on down the lane. She should have explained we will need her clothing for elimination by now."

"Little girl! Her daughter was alone in the house all night?" Fiona asked.

Rachel shook her head. "Fortunately, not. She had been staying with her grandmother for a few days. Mrs Clifton was returning her when she found her daughter."

"Mrs Clifton? Then Emily was unmarried?" Peter asked.

"There's nothing to suggest anyone else is living in the property," Rachel replied.

"My first thought is domestic violence," Peter said, walking around the body. "We'll start with finding her current boyfriend and the father of the child if it's someone different, and work from there."

Fiona stepped forward to take a quick look. The crumpled body had once been athletic. Her head was turned to the side and that side of her face was unblemished. Her mid-length, blonde hair looked professionally highlighted and cut, and her outstretched hands showed a perfect set of unchipped, painted, gel nails. Her makeup had been smudged by the rain, but the impression was of an attractive woman who took good care of her body and made the best of her looks. Looking up, she sensed Peter was impatient to leave. "Are we going to take a look inside the house?"

Peter shook his head. "We can read the report later. Our priority is finding her partner. Do you have the mother's address, Rachel?"

"Yes, it's only a five-minute walk from here. The second cottage on the right."

Peter looked towards the rear of the garden. "Anything back there?"

"We haven't had the chance to take a thorough look yet."

Peter and Fiona walked to the back of the garden. There was a small vegetable patch and a chicken run to one side. The chickens were wandering about, unfazed by events going on in the rest of the garden. On the other side, a tyre was tied to a tree branch and beside it, a wooden playhouse, complete with decking and a child's size patio set. Nothing appeared to have been disturbed, but Peter asked for a search of the entire garden to be completed.

As they removed their overalls, Rachel said, "There's one more thing before you go. It may be nothing, but John took photographs before it was bagged and removed. Next to the victim was a painted egg." Pointing, she added, "It was found over there, under the tree one end of the washing line was tied to."

"A painted egg?" Peter said, pulling a confused face. "What sort of egg?"

Fiona stepped back to view the images on the camera.

"As far as we can tell, a regular, everyday chicken egg with a face drawn on it." When Peter gave her a baffled look, Rachel added, "As I said, it might be nothing, but the face looked sinister, especially considering where it was found."

Fiona looked at the dry, dusty ground under the tree's shelter before asking to see the images of the egg where it was found.

"Looking up at Peter, Fiona said, "It does look as though it might have been placed there."

Peter gave the image a dismissive look, before saying, "The victim keeps chickens, has a young daughter, and it was Easter not long ago."

Narrowing her eyes at Peter, Fiona said, "An egg left next to a young mother with her abdomen stabbed can't be ignored."

"I didn't say it should, but there are other, far more simple explanations for the egg being there and stabbings are often to the stomach."

Fiona turned to Rachel and said, "Make sure it goes to the lab along with anything else you find. It could be entirely innocent, but it is worth checking it for fingerprints."

CHAPTER THREE

Peter stopped to sit on the bonnet of his car, looking back at the house. Fiona waited for him to catch her up, lost in her own thoughts. Maybe that egg was unrelated and had been carelessly discarded after a fun project to distract a young child, but something about it bugged her. She agreed with Rachel. The roughly drawn face did look sinister.

Impatient to move on, Fiona returned to the car. "What are you thinking?" she asked, wondering if he was having second thoughts about going inside the house, which wasn't a bad idea.

"I'm thinking I wish I smoked. Then people would assume I was having a crafty smoke without thinking about anything."

"Only, you don't smoke," Fiona pointed out. "So, what is it you're not thinking about?"

"The stabbing was erratic and carried on long after she was dead. That suggests it was someone who knew her well enough to hate her."

"That will make our job a lot easier, then," Fiona said.

"Or it could be someone who thought they knew her and what she stood for and decided to hate her for it," Peter said, pushing himself away from the car. He started to march along the lane as if it had been Fiona causing the delay.

Fiona bit her tongue, sunk her hands into her jacket pockets and started after him. Walking along the quiet lane, she thought about Peter's comment while she explained her theory about the time of death being related to the rainstorms. She knew hate and love were closely related and equally powerful emotions. Many a time, she had felt like throttling Peter.

Fiona felt a sense of the woman's vulnerability living out here alone, heightened by Emily being caught unaware while doing something so mundane as bringing in the washing. Peter could very well be correct about the culprit being close to the victim, but it was too soon to rule out alternatives. It could have been anyone from a random rambler to a disgruntled work colleague. A random attacker was the one everyone feared and would set the small, rural community on edge. Trying to reassure people that murders are rarely entirely by chance was always difficult.

"Check the times of the rainstorms when we get back to the station. As the chickens weren't put away overnight, I agree the attack was likely before nightfall," Peter said. "We can have a quick look inside the house after we have spoken to the mother and circulated details of Emily's partner and the daughter's father. If it was an unplanned attack of passion, they will be in full-panic mode trying to dispose of the evidence. The sooner we catch up with them, the better."

Peter marched purposefully through the cottage gate while Fiona took a moment to prepare herself. Speaking to the recently bereaved could be as harrowing as breaking the news of the fatality to an unsuspecting family. They would be destroying the last sliver of hope that there had been a terrible mistake. Their arrival would confirm their loved one was never coming home.

Every death and family were different, and each home held a different combination of raw emotions. Shock, denial, anger, gut-wrenching sorrow, blame and regret all displayed under the harsh, white light of a police investigation. Remnants of those emotions would settle on her clothing and be carried with her throughout the investigation.

Family and friends said she wasn't tough enough to join the police. Watching Peter confidently knock on the front door, oblivious to her over-thinking she wondered if they were right. Maybe that was why she worked so hard, never switching off from the role and denying herself a social life, to compensate.

CHAPTER FOUR

The door to a picture-book, three-storey cottage was opened by DS Abbie Ward. In a subdued tone, she said, "Come in. Melanie and Katie are through here," leading them along a short corridor to a spacious living room.

Melanie Clifton was perched on the edge of a highbacked chair, leaning forwards to watch her granddaughter crayoning in a picture book on the floor. Like her daughter, she was of athletic build, and her clothes and styled hair indicated she looked after herself and cared about her appearance. Her face was smooth, only the lines around her neck hinted at her true age.

Melanie's red-rimmed, watery eyes acknowledged their arrival, before refocussing on the purple dragon taking shape on the floor. Katie concentrated on colouring between the lines without looking up. Her face covered by a halo of blonde curls.

Fiona instinctively mirrored her colleague's muted disposition, treading carefully so as not to disturb the fragile settling of grief. Anger, blame and all the other emotions would come later. For now, the family's trauma was cloaked by a veneer of normality.

"This is DCI Hatherall and DI Williams," Abbie introduced them before gently asking, "Would Katie like to come into the kitchen with me while they ask you some questions?"

Katie stopped colouring and climbed onto her grandmother's lap. "Can I stay here with you?"

Wrapping a protective arm around Katie, Melanie said, "I don't know, darling." She looked to the officers, pleading for advice.

Fiona gave what she hoped was a reassuring smile, rather than a patronising one, to the remarkably attractive child. She didn't spend much time around children, so she had little to compare her to, but wondered if the adults' pretence of normality had gone too far. The girl seemed incredibly composed for a child who had just discovered her mother had been murdered and had possibly seen her body. "It would be for the best. We won't take too long."

"Is this about Mummy being dead?"

A chill ran down Fiona's spine when the girl's intense, blue eyes bored into her, followed by a tug at her heart. The directness of the question was so cold and matter of fact. Unsettled by the icy blue of her eyes, the perfect rosebud lips and her mop of cascading curls, a scene from *The Village of the Damned* floated into her mind. Reminding herself a child so young would not understand the concept or the permanence of death, she pushed the thought away and knelt in front of the chair. "Is that okay? We will be as quick as we can."

Katie looked up at her grandmother and back at Fiona before solemnly nodding her head and slipping down from the chair. "When are we going to Aunt Tasha's house? I like it there."

"Soon, darling," Melanie replied. "Now, run along. I will be with you in a minute."

Katie collected up her crayons and colouring book before walking over to Abbie and taking her hand.

"Such a beautiful child," Melanie said, watching her granddaughter. "So well behaved and polite."

"Would you all like a cup of tea?" Abbie asked, from the doorway.

"That would be lovely, thank you," Peter said.

Abbie led Katie from the room, asking, "Shall we look for some biscuits?"

Melanie pulled a tissue from her sleeve and dabbed at a new stream of tears. "She's our miracle child, you know."

Taking a seat, Peter asked, "How so?"

"At one point, I thought I would never be blessed with grandchildren. My oldest daughter, Tasha, discovered she couldn't have them, and we assumed it would be hereditary. Not that

I ever thought Emily would choose to start a family." Looking up, Melanie said, "Before I forget. Abbie said I should ask you. I would like to take Katie to stay with my older daughter, Tasha. Today, if possible. Will that be a problem? I don't want to stay here by myself."

"As long as we have the address and your contact details, once you've answered our questions, that will be fine," Peter replied.

"Thank you. What do you want to know?"

"I appreciate it will be difficult, but could you talk us through this morning and how you found your daughter? It was first thing this morning, I understand."

"Yes. Katie woke up early and couldn't wait to get home. I was looking after her while Emily was away on a work course for a few days. I meant to take Katie over yesterday evening as arranged, but we were late leaving Tasha's and then we were held up with traffic driving back. There was an accident, I think. Katie had fallen asleep in the car, so rather than disturb Emily, at such a late hour, I carried her up to bed here."

"Did you call your daughter to explain the change of plan?"

"It was late, so I sent her a text." Pulling out her phone, she said, "See. I sent her the text at 10.46. It says so here. It was dark by then."

Peter reached for the phone. "May I?"

Reading the text, he said, "The text wasn't seen. Were you surprised by that?"

"I assumed she was tired after her course. She knows how well I look after Katie, so she wouldn't have been worried."

"Or keen to see her after being away for several days?" After a brief silence, Peter asked, "What was your relationship with your daughter like?"

"Good. Very good. I sold my house and moved to the village when she announced she was pregnant. I've always been on hand to help as much as I can. Do you have children?"

"Yes," Peter answered quickly, ready to move on.

"So, you will understand then. My daughters' happiness is everything to me, and grandparents have such an important role to play." Glancing across at Fiona, Melanie added, "Especially as all you young women insist on having careers as well."

"Did you move here with your husband?" Peter asked, before Fiona could comment.

"My Archie passed away a good ten years ago. Such a shame he never met Katie. He would have adored her. Everyone does."

Peter exchanged a look with Fiona. She wasn't sure if it related to the comment about careers or whether he noticed that Melanie repeatedly praised her granddaughter rather than dwell on the loss of her daughter.

"Do you know where Emily's work course was?"

"Sorry, you'll have to ask the school. Emily is … was a teacher at the village primary school. Katie goes there as well."

"We'll check with them later," Peter said. "What can you tell me about Katie's father?"

"Absolutely nothing." Melanie stood up from her chair and crossed the room to a side cabinet. "It's the Saturday after half-term. There will be nobody at the school. The headmistress is called Judy Devoto." Opening a drawer, she said, "I'm sure I have her number in here, somewhere. Emily gave it to me when she started working at the school in case there was an emergency."

"What sort of emergency was she imagining?" Peter asked, his eyes following Melanie across the room.

"No idea, but that is typical Emily. She likes everyone to be prepared for all eventualities." After rummaging through the drawer, Melanie returned to her chair with a slim diary. "Well? Do you want her number?"

As Fiona scribbled the number in her notepad, Peter asked, "Do you have the contact details for Katie's father?"

"No," Melanie said, closing the diary. "Emily never told anyone who he was. She said it wasn't important. A careless, one-night stand. Coming just after Tasha learned she could never have children it was quite a shock for all of us. Tasha took the news hard, and they haven't spoken since. I always hoped they would make up and be friends again." Melanie's lips quivered before she added, "And now it's too late," before burrowing her head in her hands.

Abbie walked in carrying a tray of mugs. Katie followed with a smaller tray holding a selection of biscuits. Melanie raised her head and forced a smile for her granddaughter before taking a biscuit from the tray. "Thank you, darling."

"Are you okay, Granny?" Katie asked, nearly tipping the tray on the floor, as she rubbed her grandmother's arm, looking concerned.

"Yes, yes. I'm fine. I'm just being silly. Are you having fun in the kitchen?"

"Yes!" Katie replied, the look of concern disappearing in a flash. "Abbie drew me a picture of a pony, and I'm colouring it in for you. Can I have a pony? It could live on Aunt Tasha's farm. Please."

"We'll see," Melanie said.

Katie offered Peter a biscuit, then carefully balancing the tray, crossed the room to Fiona. Taking a homemade flapjack, Fiona said, "Thank you, Katie. This looks delicious. Did you help to make them?" When Katie nodded and gave an angelic smile, Fiona asked, "Do you help to look after the chickens in your garden?"

Katie's head bobbed up and down so much, she nearly dropped the remaining biscuits in Fiona's lap. "I help feed them and collect the eggs."

"Careful, darling," Melanie said, as Katie's tray tilted downwards. Tearing her eyes from her granddaughter, she said, "That reminds me. Before we leave, I'll call my friend in the village to feed the chickens and lock them up at night. Will that be okay?"

"Give your friend's name to Abbie, and I'm sure that can be cleared," Peter said.

Helping Katie rebalance the plate, Fiona asked, "Do you sometimes draw faces on the eggs?"

Katie guiltily looked at the floor but didn't reply.

"Don't you remember?" Melanie said. "We painted lots of eggs for Easter."

Katie looked up at Fiona through her impossibly long eyelashes before stepping back and taking Abbie's hand, indicating she wanted to return to the kitchen.

Melanie took a sip of tea before putting it to one side with the uneaten biscuit. Shaking her head at the closed door to the kitchen, she said, "A pony. Whatever next?"

"You said there was some ill-feeling between your daughters after Emily fell pregnant," Peter said, obviously keen to get the interview back on track.

"Not really. More of a silence. It was Susan I expected to be more upset. As it turned out, she took it all in her stride. She doted on Katie as much as Emily. If it caused a rift in their relationship, it didn't show."

"Susan? Who is Susan?"

"Up until a few months ago, Emily's partner. They've been together for nearly eight years." Melanie's hands shot to her mouth. "I'm going to have to break the news to her. She'll be devastated. Emily wouldn't talk about why they split, but I assumed they would get back together. They were so similar in looks and personality. Maybe that was the problem." Melanie stopped talking, and a look of horror spread across her face. "Will she have custody rights? Could she take Katie away? Emily would never have wanted that. Katie belongs here, with me."

"If you pass her details to Fiona, we can contact Susan," Peter said.

"Oh, could you?" Melanie asked, looking relieved before re-opening her diary. "I would contact her myself, but I need to focus all my energy on little Katie. I don't think I have the capacity to deal with Susan's grief on top of everything else. If she should ask, will you stress Katie is safe and well with me? Where she should be."

"Child custody isn't our domain." Clearing his throat, Peter said, "We think it's possible your daughter's attacker was someone known to her."

Instantly twigging what Peter was suggesting, Melanie said, "No, not Susan. She would never harm Emily. No matter what. She will be heartbroken by the news. My only concern is she might want to hang on to Katie for all the wrong reasons. Katie belongs here. With her family."

Acknowledging Melanie's opinion with a nod, Peter asked, "What does she do for a living?"

"She's a doctor of something or other. Not a medical one, you understand. She works at Birstall University, running a research programme into sleep disorders." Melanie firmly added, "So you see, not the sort of person to do anything violent. She was an academic. She has letters after her name. But it also means she is far too busy to look after an active child."

"Did your daughter have any new relationships recently?"

"No ... but she never went away on weekends before Susan left. I didn't like to pry, but I have wondered if maybe she was meeting someone else. I considered finding an excuse to introduce myself to Judy so I could ask her about the work course. Emily told me to leave her alone, and if I'm honest, I'm not sure I would go behind my daughter's back to check up on her. But I would be lying if I said I wasn't tempted."

"Judy? That's the headmistress?" When Melanie nodded, Peter asked, "Do you have her address?"

"Oh, yes. She moved into Dee's old place on the high street a few months ago. It's two doors down from The Lamb Inn, called Lilac Cottage."

"Can you think of anyone your daughter had an argument with recently?"

"No. Emily lived a quiet life, and everyone loved her."

"No enemies at all?" When Melanie shook her head, Peter said, "How about ex-partners? Somebody who maybe loved her too much?"

"I can't think of anyone like that. Emily and Susan were completely devoted to one another. That's why Susan leaving was such a surprise. There was no warning. One day she was here, and the next, she was gone."

"Okay. That will be all for now. You'll leave full details of where we can contact you with Abbie?"

"Will do."

CHAPTER FIVE

Outside, Fiona called the number for Susan Penrose. Taking the phone away from her ear, she said, "Either I've written it down wrong, or the number Melanie gave me, no longer exists." Before Peter could respond, Fiona was already speaking to Abbie. "Could you ask Melanie for Susan Penrose's telephone number again? And whether she has tried to ring the number recently." Walking as she listened, Fiona ended the call. "I rang the correct number. She hasn't spoken to Susan since they split up, but she has contacted her on the number before."

Peter speeded up his walk. "I don't like the sound of that." Instead of entering Emily's driveway, he walked past the parked cars and unlocked his. "I'll ring the station to make sure they've made a start on tracking her down." Climbing into the seat, he said, "Ring the headmistress. I want to know where she was this week. The team will be at the house all day. We can come back here after we've spoken to her."

They were unable to find a space to park in the narrow street outside Lilac Cottage, so Peter pulled into the car park behind the Lamb Inn. Unbuckling his seat belt, he said, "You know what this means?"

"Wild stab in the dark. We'll be having lunch here," Fiona replied, climbing out of the car. The not drinking on duty memos were clearly still going in the bin.

Judy Devoto was not the homely village headmistress they

had expected. She was tall and athletic looking. Good health and vitality sprang from every pore as she invited them in. The cottage was decorated with a jumble of traditional, quaint, English touches and obscure, stone artefacts, most of which were strangely erotic. The living room walls were painted bright orange, with one wall dominated by a brightly coloured tapestry. Crossing the room, Peter and Fiona dodged numerous plants trailing from pots attached to the ceiling by a complex network of chains. Relieved to have made it across the room without suffering a concussion, they sank into luxurious armchairs after declining refreshments.

Judy, dressed in flamboyant, purple leggings and an oversized, man's button-down shirt, sat cross-legged on the floor in front of them. An exotic-looking, silver cat slinked from behind a statue of a couple making love and crawled onto her lap. Stroking the cat, Judy joked, "For what do I owe the pleasure of Her Majesty's finest? I am here entirely legally."

"We've come from Emily Clifton's home," Peter said.

"Oh, yes, Emily," Judy said, in a dismissive tone. "A good teacher, but she never struck me as the adventurous type. What on earth has she been up to?"

"I'm afraid she was found dead this morning," Peter said.

Judy's hands shot to her mouth as her eyes widened in horror. "Oh, no! How terrible." She stood up, pushing the disgruntled cat to the floor, and moved to an armchair. Her eyes watered as she patted her chest. "Sorry. Excuse me for a moment. This is such a shock." She closed her eyes and inhaled and exhaled several times to calm herself. Opening her eyes, she asked, "Was it a stupid accident? Or a stroke or something like that? I always thought her a little tense. Being so uptight is not good for your health." Opening her arms wide, she added, "It is important to be open to life and to breathe deeply."

"No. Miss Clifton was murdered," Peter said.

Judy's arms dropped to her side. "Murdered?" she repeated, her eyebrows almost levitating above her forehead. "But why?"

"That's what we're hoping to find out," Peter said. "Were you close?"

"I take an interest in all my staff. A feeling of communal wellness can only improve the educational experience, but I wouldn't say I was *close* with Emily. I'm not sure anyone was. Whenever we spoke, I always felt something was blocking her energy."

"Such as?"

Judy shrugged. "Sorry, I knew little of her private life or what may have caused the blockage. It was just an impression I had."

"Other than having blocked energy, how would you describe Emily?"

"Katie! Her little girl? Is she …?"

"She spent the evening with her grandmother, so she is unharmed," Peter reassured her.

"That's a blessing. Such a sweet, little girl. Very bright."

"She still has the trauma of losing her mother to contend with," Peter reminded Judy. "Emily told her mother she was attending a work course this week. Can you tell us where there was?"

Judy's brows furrowed in confusion. "Work course? That's the first I've heard of it. What sort of course?"

"So, it wasn't something arranged by the school?"

"Absolutely not," Judy replied. "I have no idea why she would have claimed it was."

"What can you tell us about Emily?" When Judy looked blank, Peter prompted, "What she was like? Who were her friends?"

"She was a caring mother and an excellent teacher. The children loved her and did well in her class."

"But?" Peter asked. "I sense there's a but."

"She didn't join in with school social events unless coerced to attend. I felt she was over-protective towards Katie." Sighing, Judy said, "You're bound to find out sooner or later. There was an incident at the end of last year."

"Go on. What sort of incident?"

"It was something of nothing that was blown out of all proportion. I apologised for the mistake and assured her it wouldn't happen again, but still, she was very aggressive towards me and another teacher. It was out of character for her, and we wondered if something was going on in her private life to make her overreact the way she did. It hasn't been mentioned again, so I assume it had all blown over. Not that I think it could have anything to do with her being murdered."

"I'll be the judge of that. Would you like to explain this incident?" Peter asked.

"Yes, yes. Of course. Although I doubt it is relevant. As you may be aware, there are strict rules about photographing children. Parents can request no images of their children are taken or used in any way. Last Christmas, Katie was Mary in our nativity play. Because of Covid restrictions, only one adult per child was able to watch the scaled-down performance. A photograph of the scene around the crib was published in the local newspaper. Emily was livid as she had forbidden the use of her daughter's image. It was a simple oversight by the class teacher, and I authorised it without checking. In my opinion, Emily should have realised the risk when Katie was chosen for the role and highlighted her concerns then. As well as being abusive towards the teacher, Mr Jenkins, she threatened to sue the school and me personally."

"And did she? Sue the school or anyone else, that is," Peter asked.

"No. Things calmed down after the holidays, and it is all water under the bridge, now. I thought I should mention it, rather than you hear about it from someone else, and go thinking I had something to hide. I asked her at the time if anything else was causing her stress, and she told me to mind my own business. Like I said earlier, she did seem to be quite an uptight person."

"Thank you for that. How did she get on with the other teachers?"

"I'm not aware of any issues. She had a good working relationship with everyone, including Mr Jenkins, both before and after the incident. Although we always had to make sure we updated her. We have a Facebook group. Emily was the only member of staff who didn't join."

"We would like to speak to the teachers, especially Mr Jenkins, next week when the school is open. Will that be a problem?"

"Of course not. Like me, I am sure all the staff will want to do everything they can to help. If you call ahead to pre-warn me, I can make myself available to cover any necessary absences from class while the interviews take place to minimize any disruption."

CHAPTER SIX

Back in the car, Peter returned a missed call to the station. "They've drawn a complete blank on tracing Susan Penrose. No forwarding address or social media accounts. She told the university she needed some time away from everything and has completely disappeared. I'm assuming, *'the everything,'* was referring to the relationship breaking down, but we need to check there wasn't something else going on."

"Even so, somebody must know where she went," Fiona said.

"We could try the university, but it's probably only skeleton staff over the weekend."

"It still might be worth a try. What about Emily's social media accounts? Can they trace anything from them?" Fiona suggested.

"Emily deleted all of her accounts about seven years ago."

"Interesting. How old do you think Emily's daughter is? I'm not great on children's ages, but I would say she's six or seven. That would mean Emily deleted her accounts around the time of her pregnancy. I wonder if there may have been something more to the nativity play fiasco. Despite all the warnings, my Facebook feed is full of pictures of my friends' children. As soon as they fall pregnant, they become obsessed with posting every milestone of their child's life, no matter how small or insignificant. Yet, Emily appears to have done the exact opposite. Most parents would be overjoyed to see their precious child in the newspaper with a starring role. Even if it was only the school nativity. Emily seems to have gone to a great deal of trouble to hide her pregnancy and her daughter."

"One explanation would be she didn't want the father to find out," Peter said. "Which makes it doubly important we track down Susan. If she's not the culprit, she's the one person who might know who Katie's father is."

"Maybe the father discovered the pregnancy, so Emily arranged a meeting when she knew Katie wouldn't be around? And he became violent when she said she would deny him access? A history of violence could explain why Emily was so keen to keep her pregnancy quiet and keep a low profile on social media," Fiona said. "If that's the case, her telephone records will help us."

"I doubt she would have invited him to her home if she intended to deny access. She would have arranged the meeting somewhere miles away. Giving him her address would have been the last thing she would have done."

"Maybe he had already traced her address and turned up unexpectedly? Or, she arranged to meet him elsewhere, and he followed her back," Fiona replied.

"What did you make of Melanie?"

"She's clearly fond of Katie and gave the impression of the perfect mother and grandmother, but …. Don't you think it strange that Emily lied about a school course when it could be so easily disproved?"

"She would have known her mother better than anyone. Maybe she knew she wouldn't check up on her."

"Possibly, but I still feel there's something not quite right," Fiona said. "She's awfully keen to have custody of Katie."

"She's in shock having just lost her daughter. I would say that's a normal reaction for a grandparent who is healthy and has been involved from day one."

"You might be right," Fiona said, thinking about her parents and their increasing neediness as their health faltered. If something happened to her brother, they would want to retain contact with their grandchildren but wouldn't take full responsibility for them. They would expect her to. If there was nobody else, she would try her best, but it would be a struggle and not an undertaking she would take on lightly. She conceded, her family circumstances were different. Melanie was fit and healthy and devoted to her family. But she thought her parents would be too devastated at the loss of their favourite child to be thinking about custody battles.

"Let's grab something to eat in the pub, then we'll see if anything of interest has turned up at the house. If we haven't heard back with an address for Susan, we'll head out to the university on the chance we can find someone who knows where she is."

◆ ◆ ◆

The team were still working methodically through the house when Peter and Fiona finished their lunch and returned. The kitchen drawers had been wrenched out, and the contents emptied onto the floor. It looked like the intruder had been searching for something specific. The open handbag remained on the kitchen table, although it was currently in a sealed plastic bag. Fiona caught the attention of a white-clad woman holding a clipboard in the hallway. "Do you know if a mobile phone or a diary was found in the handbag?"

The woman flicked through some sheets attached to her clipboard. "No. Inside the bag, there was a purse containing cash and credit cards, makeup, sweet wrappers, a romance novel and her car keys." She flicked over the pages and said, "Two laptops were found upstairs. They have been removed to be checked, but no mobile phone has been found. One thing that may interest you. In the purse was a return train ticket from Oxford used yesterday."

"Thank you," Fiona said, already scrolling through contacts on her mobile. "Hi Abbie, it's me again. Could you ask Melanie who Emily knew in Oxford? We think that was where she was the last few days."

Waiting for Abbie to obtain the information, Fiona followed Peter up the stairs. Evidence of a frantic search was everywhere, and the SOCO team were scurrying around recording everything. Stepping over the scattered, manila files covering the landing, she followed Peter's lead, poking her head into each room, being careful not to touch anything. The damage to what she assumed was Katie's bedroom was extensive. Books and cuddly toys had been swiped from the shelves, and a dolls house and its contents had been reduced to splinters of wood. The duvet had been thrown from the bed and the mattress slashed by a knife.

"I think we've seen enough in here for now," Peter said. "They'll contact us if they find her mobile."

Abbie reappeared on the line as Fiona walked down the stairs and through the kitchen. She glanced out of the kitchen window at two officers on hands and knees examining the ground near the washing line. As they reached the front door, Fiona said, "Melanie has just left for her other daughter's home. Before she left, she said she had no idea who her daughter may have been visiting in Oxford."

"We'll head up to Birstall University, now. Get onto Oxford station to obtain CCTV from the train station. It's in an awkward position out on the ring road. We might get lucky and see her meeting someone or getting into a car."

The university campus was eerily quiet as Peter and Fiona made their way to the research centre. It was a modern, hexagon-shaped building with a formal garden at the side. A couple of students shared a coffee on one of the benches, but otherwise, the area was deserted. They located the office for Dr Penrose, exchanging looks at her nameplate still attached to the door before knocking.

Inside, they were greeted by Margaret Adegboyega. She was quick to reassure them that she was fully competent to lead the current research programme in Susan's absence.

"It is the whereabouts of Dr Penrose we are interested in, rather than your work here," Peter said.

Fiona wasn't so sure they should be so dismissive of Susan's work but held her tongue. The woman seemed overly defensive. It could be to mask insecurity in her temporary role or be something more.

"I'm afraid I do not know where she is," Margaret said. "We have been working very intensely, and she requested a full break. She didn't tell anyone where she was going. I gained the impression, she might be travelling around from place to place."

"Surely you have a contact number for her. What if a serious problem cropped up?" Peter asked.

"I can't imagine a scenario I wouldn't be able to handle. Our current research project is nearly complete. It is merely a case of following up on our participants and collating all the information."

"You said, Dr Penrose requested a full break. Had she been under a great deal of stress?" Peter asked. "Either here or at home."

"Causes of stress are varied and subjective. We have been busy with tight time deadlines. Maybe it was getting to her. I'm afraid I know nothing about her home life. If there were issues there, she never brought them into work with her."

"Did you know she broke up with her partner recently?" Fiona asked.

"I think I did hear something about it. We weren't close friends, just work colleagues, so she never confided in me."

"Who funds your research?" Fiona asked. "Pharmaceutical companies presumably, testing new sleep medication."

Margaret nodded. "Considering we spend so much time asleep, surprisingly little is known about it. Our recent work has been funded by Astra Zeneca. They wished to know how sleep deprivation would affect the production of antibodies following vaccination."

Suddenly, more interested, Peter asked, "Would Dr Penrose have needed to meet with company representatives?"

"A couple of times, and they have visited us here."

"Could we have the contact details of those representatives?" Peter asked.

Margaret's eyes narrowed and she folded her arms. "You haven't explained your interest in tracing Dr Penrose. Is she in some sort of trouble? I can assure you all the work we carry out here is fully regulated and to a high standard."

"I'm sure it is. We are investigating the murder of a close friend of hers. It is important we speak to her as soon as possible," Peter replied.

"How dreadful, but I'm not sure how you think the company funding our research could be of any help to you. Any contact would have been purely professional."

"The friend had just returned from a trip to Oxford."

Margaret smiled and shook her head, before replying, "Then there is no connection. Astra Zeneca has its UK head office in Cambridge."

"But it's called the Oxford Astra Zeneca vaccine," Peter protested.

"They collaborated with the Jennings Institute, which is connected to Oxford University. Their labs are based in Headington, a few miles outside of Oxford. We dealt with personnel from Cambridge, and I'm not prepared to divulge their details on the basis of such a spurious connection."

"This is a murder investigation."

"I'm not denying that, but I fail to see there's any connection to the work carried out here," Margaret said firmly. "I'm not stopping you from contacting the Jennings Institute direct, but I'm sure they will be as flummoxed by the request as I am."

The office door opened, and a young woman with spiked, dyed hair stumbled into the room.

"Pippa! Did you want something?" Margaret asked sharply.

"Umm, yes, but it's not important. I'll come back later."

Before the young woman could retreat from the room, Fiona asked, "Are you involved in the sleep trials being carried out here?"

"Umm. Yes," the student replied.

"Did you have any contact with Dr Penrose? We're trying to track her down."

"Umm. Some. Yeah. But I have no idea where she is. Sorry."

"I'll see you later," Margaret said. As the girl left, closing the door behind her, Margaret stood. "If that is all, I have work to complete."

"For now," Peter said, also standing.

"I would prefer it if you didn't speak to the students without clearing it with me first," Margaret said, determined to have the last word.

◆ ◆ ◆

Peter grumbled about Margaret's attitude all the way back to the car. Before starting the car, he called the station for an update. "Nothing much to report," he said, ending the call. "I may as well drop you off back home. Details of the murder will be going out on the local and national news tonight. If Susan calls in afterwards, will you be available?"

"Of course," Fiona replied, pulling out her phone to text Stefan to say she was on her way.

CHAPTER SEVEN

Fiona closed her eyes and counted to ten when she walked through her front door. A huge bouquet of flowers stood on the hallway table, and she could smell something delicious cooking in the kitchen. She opened the door to the dining room and poked her head in. The table was fully set, and lit candles flickered from every surface as Ed Sheeran played from the surround speakers.

She closed the door and examined the flowers, rubbing her forehead in frustration. As soon as news of Emily's death went out on the national news, Susan was bound to contact the station. Checking the hallway clock, she estimated Peter would call her somewhere between the main course and dessert. Hardly the romantic evening Stefan had planned for them.

"In here!"

Sighing, Fiona picked up her bag and opened the kitchen door. As she walked in, her phone rang. Dropping her bag on a kitchen chair and pulling out her phone, she started to word her explanation to Stefan for having to go straight back out. After her initial confusion, she said, "Hi, Mum."

Listening to her mother, she waved away the offered glass of white wine and pulled out a can of lemonade from the fridge. She concentrated on the call, avoiding eye contact with Stefan, who leant on the counter sipping from a wine glass. After waiting patiently for her mother's tale of woe to end, she said, "That doesn't sound good, but you need to call a heating engineer, not me … Where's Dad? … Wake him up and ask him for the number of the firm you use … Okay … Let me know when someone is coming out to you."

Stefan reoffered the wine glass as Fiona ended the call and returned her phone to her open bag. "Oh, Stefan. I'm sorry. I can't drink tonight. I will be driving back to the station later."

"But you have just come in."

"I know. I know. It's just the way things are. Early on in a case, things happen quickly, and I have to be there when they do."

"You will have time to eat?"

"Yes, hopefully. It smells wonderful."

Throughout the meal, Fiona was on tenterhooks expecting Peter's call any minute. Her mother called back to say a plumber arrived, but there was nothing from Peter. His call came as they were finishing dessert.

Without preamble, Peter said, "She hasn't rung in. The news bulletins went out nearly an hour ago. And there is something else. The records show she graduated from Manchester University as Catherine Susan Penrose."

"So? A lot of people choose to use their second name."

"Catherine Penrose died in a car accident before taking up her place at university."

"Oh. Should I come in?"

"Everything possible is being done to find her. Get an early night, and we'll make a fresh start tomorrow morning. Meet at seven o'clock?"

"It's Sunday, tomorrow."

"Okay. Seven-thirty. See you then."

Fiona glared at her phone screen that had gone dead.

"Problem?" Stefan asked.

"Maybe, but nothing can be done tonight. Is there still some wine left?"

CHAPTER EIGHT

Nursing a sore head, Fiona entered the near-empty, operations room, bang on seven-thirty. Abbie Ward was on the telephone with her back to her. Phil Humphries looked up from behind his computer screen and waved. Peter appeared by her side and handed over a shop-bought coffee and pastry from the Squire Inn in the high street.

Fiona took a grateful sip of the coffee. "How's it looking this morning?"

"Still no contact as far as I can tell. I was about to ask Abbie whether anyone had tracked Susan down overnight when her phone rang."

"I'm pretty sure they didn't," Humphries said, standing up to stretch. "They didn't find anything helpful at the house either, other than the train ticket."

Abbie ended her call, and said, "It's like Susan Penrose disappeared off the planet when she left the area. Car sold, bank accounts closed, mobile disconnected. We're getting nowhere."

"Interesting," Fiona said, forgetting her intention to take another couple of painkillers with her coffee. "Do we know when she and Emily got together? We assumed Emily closed all her social media accounts when she fell pregnant. Maybe it was more to do with Susan wanting to stay completely off the radar."

"To protect her false identity," Peter said.

Humphries checked his computer screen, before saying, "They were together for two years before Katie was born, give or take a few months."

"Which is it? Give or take?" Peter asked sharply. "A pregnancy takes nine months the last time I looked. Fiona could be onto something."

Humphries returned to his screen and tapped a few keys before saying, "Susan wasn't officially registered as living with Emily, so there is no set date to work from. Friends say they hit it off as soon as they met, and it was roughly another six months until she moved in."

"Can you see if you can get something more definite from Emily's mother?" Fiona asked. "It would be helpful to know if she closed the social media accounts to keep the relationship or the pregnancy a secret."

"It could be both," Abbie pointed out. Turning her attention to her computer screen, she added, "There's another couple of things I want to try before giving up."

"Could Susan be using her real name?" DC Andrew Litton asked, as he entered the room and headed for his desk.

"Possibly, but as we have no idea what it is, it's not a lot of help," Peter said. "There's a coffee for you on the side. How did you and Eddie fare with the neighbours yesterday?"

"Nothing of note. Emily was universally described as quiet and polite," Andrew replied, collecting his coffee.

"When Eddie finally arrives, interview the teachers at Brierley school. Emily had a disagreement with one of the teachers. It's all in the case file. He will need to provide an alibi. Let me know what you think of him and any other discrepancies that crop up," Peter said.

Fiona started on her pastry while waiting for her computer screen to wake up.

Peter said, "Time is slipping away from us. She may be innocent, but if she isn't, we're giving Susan, or whatever her real name is, far too much time to cover up the evidence and leave the country."

"How sure are you that she was responsible for the attack?" Humphries asked.

"I'm not sure of anything yet," Peter said. "I'm trying to keep an open mind, but Susan's history, or lack of it and her failure to contact us voluntarily, is closing it. Most murders are carried out by someone close to the victim. Maybe Emily discovered Susan wasn't who she said she was."

"Unrequited love is high on the list of reasons for murder. It might be they were discussing custody of Katie at a time Emily knew Katie wouldn't be there," Humphries said.

"Except, Melanie said they were unexpectedly delayed. Katie should have been there," Fiona pointed out. "There was a major accident on the Alderston road. They would have been coming from that direction, so it is likely they would have been caught up in the aftermath, as she said."

"Or irritation," Humphries said.

Fiona gave Humphries a quizzical look, while Peter asked, "What are you on about?"

"When family members and friends kill each other, it's often due to irritation. You hear it all the time. He was slurping his tea or eating with his mouth open when I've asked him a hundred times before not to. Something snapped, and I lashed out."

Fiona turned away to hide a chuckle that threatened to erupt at the withering stare Peter was giving Humphries before he muttered, "Irritation as a defence. I'll be sure to remember that in case I have to rely on it after a *staff incident*."

Humphries winked at Fiona as Peter stomped across the room to look out of the window before turning to sit on the windowsill. Fiona raised her eyebrows at Humphries before she wandered across to look at the crime scene photographs attached to the whiteboard.

Peter probably spent the night checking his phone to see if Susan had been in contact. Needling him when he was tired and grumpy wasn't going to end well for any of them.

Humphries was like an oversized, annoying child at times. She was never sure whether he meant to cause friction, or if he thought he was being funny. Occasionally, she wondered whether he thought at all. But when it mattered, he concentrated, and he was a good detective and a loyal friend. They both were, and she didn't want to be stuck between the pair of them arguing.

Ignoring Humphries rolling his eyes, she pinned a photograph of the painted egg to the board. The more she looked at it, the more menacing the roughly drawn face looked. It looked too staged with its face turned upwards to have been accidentally dropped there, another time. Sighing, she recrossed the room to the desk nearest the window.

When she pulled out a chair, Peter said, "I have a bad feeling about Susan going to such lengths to hide her whereabouts. We haven't found anything to say who she really was, so we have no family history, or anything else useful to help us find her. She appeared from nowhere shortly before meeting Emily and has now disappeared back there. Only, we are clueless as to where there is. I know academics become totally absorbed in their work, and even if the name change is incidental, she must have seen the news bulletins last night."

"Or," Fiona said, tapping her fingers on the desk to play for time while she organised her thoughts. "What if Susan had a good reason to hide her identity and she was the intended victim? Emily died refusing to give up her whereabouts, and Susan is now running scared."

"Then, it's even more important she contacts us. We can protect her."

Fiona turned her chair to face the desk, thinking over possible reasons for Susan's lack of contact. It could be related to anything from her old identity to her current work. The sleep research programme at the local university seemed mainstream and uncontroversial, but it could be a cover for something else. Something that led to the murder.

Andrew was still settling himself at his desk, while Peter and Humphries seemed content to sit with their own thoughts waiting for Abbie to work her magic on the internet. Fiona logged onto her computer to read through the overnight reports to check she was up to date.

The silence was disturbed by Rachel Mann's entrance with a cheery hello. "The initial reports have just come in from the laptops found at the house. By the looks of it, Susan Penrose was looking at job opportunities in America," she said, handing a thin file to Peter.

After flicking through the contents, Peter said, "Her searches started six months ago."

"It could be what caused the split," Andrew said.

"And explain why she hasn't been in contact. She may be attending an interview in the States for all we know," Humphries said.

"We know she hasn't left the country since the attack," Peter said. "Check how far back we searched. Although, if she has a passport in her real name, that won't help us much. What name was she using to apply for the positions?"

"Dr Catherine Susan Penrose. Is there anything I can do?" Rachel asked.

"Yes," Fiona said. "Can you chase up what happened to the egg that was found next to Emily? I don't see any mention of it here."

"A child drawing faces on eggs is hardly unheard of. Especially if she had recently been painting them with her grandmother," Humphries said.

Peter looked across at Abbie, and asked, "Anything yet?"

Abbie shook her head and held up her hand with five fingers spread out, indicating they had another few minutes to wait.

"I think the best way to find Susan is to speak to their mutual friends and her university colleagues," Peter said. "They should know whether she was seriously considering a move to America and Emily's reaction to the idea. We might discover Susan had a jealous streak, and she took the break-up of the relationship badly. Chances are she let something slip that would give us a clue as to where she is."

Following a brief pause, Humphries said, "Maybe Susan wasn't as happy with the one-night stand as Melanie suggested. Or she discovered Emily had continued a friendship with the father behind her back."

Fiona blocked out their speculation while thoughts of the egg nagged away at her. The face was crudely drawn and could have been done by a child. She wished Katie had given a proper answer. Her guilty look when she had asked her was hardly conclusive. Concentrating on her own train of thought, she returned to her search of the national database.

Abbie pushed her chair back from the desk in frustration. "Sorry, guys. I've got nothing for you. I haven't a clue who Susan might be or where she has disappeared."

Peter slid off the windowsill. "I want to interview their mutual friends before heading back to the university. She must have confided in one of them."

"What about Emily's sister?" Andrew asked, raising an eyebrow at Humphries. "Hadn't they irritated each other and fallen out?"

"Hang on a minute," Fiona said, not looking up from the screen. "I might have something here. Three weeks ago, a doctor working at a fertility clinic in Silton was murdered in her kitchen. There were multiple stab wounds to her abdomen in what was described as a violent and chaotic attack. The house was ransacked, but no fingerprints were found. Despite the damage caused, nothing was taken even though cash and jewellery were easily accessible. The woman lived a quiet, unassuming life with her partner of thirty years. The attack happened when the partner was away visiting a sick relative. Silton station are working on the basis that the attack related to her work as they have drawn a complete blank on any personal motive."

"Why do you think the two cases are connected?" Peter asked.

"Don't tell me she liked to decorate eggs," Humphries said.

Ignoring Humphries, Fiona said, "A knife identical to the one left at our scene was found on the kitchen floor. Silton is just outside of our area. The style of attack and the trashing of the house sound similar. The couple were described as quiet and unassuming, and the partner's alibi checked out. Without any suspects or motives, their theory is the attacker has a serious problem with the science of helping couples to conceive."

Peter sat back down on the window ledge, rubbing his chin, deep in thought.

Humphries stood up to rotate neck, and said, "If Emily became pregnant after a one-night stand, I think we can safely say she had no fertility issues."

"But her sister does," Fiona said.

All heads turned as a breathless DC Eddie Jordan barrelled through the door, waving a sheet of paper. Catching his breath, he said, "Sorry, I'm late. I picked this up on my way through. A neighbour called to say she spotted a stranger leaving Melanie Clifton's house. The possible intruder left the house on foot, but a short while later, the neighbour heard what she thought was a motorcycle engine starting up. The neighbour didn't want to take a closer look because of what happened to her daughter."

"Melanie took Katie to stay with her other daughter, didn't she?" Peter asked.

"Yes. They left late afternoon, yesterday," Fiona confirmed.

Peter turned to Abbie. "Can you come with me to interview the friends and work colleagues?" When Abbie nodded, he turned to Fiona and said, "Take Humphries with you to check out the house. It could have been someone from the tabloids sniffing out a story. When you update Melanie, you can check for any family connection with this fertility clinic. Take things from there but let me know what's going on. Eddie, you're with Andrew at Brierly village school."

CHAPTER NINE

The small, close-knit group of friends Emily and Susan shared gave the same story of a quiet, devoted couple with a perfect life of domestic bliss. They perceived them to be the ideal couple, and they had never witnessed any behaviour to suggest jealousy or possessiveness. The break-up had come as a complete shock to all of them. After failing to contact Susan, they had rallied around Emily who refused to discuss why Susan had suddenly left. They confirmed both women doted on Katie, who had never been the cause of any friction in the relationship, and Melanie was the perfect grandmother, always on hand to help financially as well as practically.

To Peter, the domestic situation sounded too impossibly perfect to be true. There again, he conceded, his view was based on his experience of one chaotic, failed relationship after another.

The picture-perfect image of family life was tarnished when Peter and Abbie met Allison, the last of Emily's friends on their list. She had completed her teaching training with Emily, and they had shared a house in their final year. She taught in a secondary school several miles away, but she caught up with Emily every few months during the school holidays. She had only met Susan briefly, so was unable to comment on their relationship other than to say Emily seemed happy, and she was adamant that Emily would want Katie to be with Susan, not with her witch of a mother.

"Why do you say that?" Peter asked. "We've been led to believe Emily had an enviable, close relationship with her mother. Melanie moved house to be on hand to help as much as could."

Allison gave an impressive eye roll. "That's the impression Melanie likes to give. Emily felt trapped. Her mother was always interfering and criticising her. All the help her mother gave was conditional on her dictating how they led their lives."

"Why didn't Emily put a stop to it if she felt that suffocated by her mother?" Abbie asked.

"We discussed just that. Endlessly. Emily knew she was too dependent on Melanie, and she was trying to change things. I last saw her over the Christmas holidays. I know under the Covid rules we shouldn't have, but we were both teaching classes of thirty-plus students every day. To say we shouldn't meet up with friends seemed ridiculous. Emily told me that week that she was making plans with Susan that didn't involve her mother. I took that to mean they were going to bite the bullet and set up home somewhere else. Unfortunately, she called to cancel our meeting planned for this Easter."

"Did Emily mention them moving to America?" Abbie asked.

"She didn't, but that wouldn't surprise me. Emily has always been good at keeping things close to her chest. I certainly had the impression that where they were going, Melanie would find it hard to follow."

"Did you know she had split up with Susan?"

"No, I didn't. Not until … recently … since her death. When I first heard it on the news, a small part of me thought that Melanie had gotten wind of their plans and put a stop to them. But that can't be right, can it? She was elsewhere, looking after Katie."

"How well do you know Melanie?" Peter asked.

"I met her a few times when I shared a house with Emily. And of course, at our graduation party. I think it was because I wasn't in contact with her mother that Emily felt she could confide in me how she really felt. Do you know about, *'The Episode?'* When Emily and Katie stayed here a short while?"

"No, tell us more."

"Emily was suffering from postnatal depression, which accentuated the problem, but the undercurrent never went away." Allison took a deep breath before plunging into the story. "Shortly after Katie was born, Emily turned up here with Katie, late one night. She was hysterical. Convinced her mother wanted to steal Katie from her and asking me to keep them hidden. Once she had seen a doctor and was given medication, things settled down. After a few weeks, Susan took them home. While Emily accepted things had gotten out of proportion, she told me on several other occasions that her mother wanted Katie to herself."

Digesting that information, Peter asked, "Have you any idea who Katie's father might be?"

"I can't say for sure, and she denied it, but I always wondered if it might have been Carston."

"Carston? Who is he?" Peter asked.

"He was a German exchange teacher at my school. He was supposed to stay for the full year, but there was a family emergency of some description, and he left after only one term. I introduced him to Emily when he first arrived, and they seemed to get along. A week or so later, I bumped into them having lunch together at a riverside pub out Berth way. She said she was just being hospitable as she figured he hadn't had time to make any friends, but I had the feeling there was more to it." After a brief silence, Allison said, "He was tall, muscular and blond with piercing, blue eyes. I won't lie, I found him very attractive, and I was a tiny, bit jealous. I was under the impression things were already serious with Susan, so I wasn't sure what she was playing at. Having a final fling with a guy?" Shrugging, Allison added, "Who knows?"

"Do you have any idea where he is now?" Peter asked.

"Back in Germany, I guess. Probably married with a couple of children. I didn't keep in contact, but the school might know how to contact him." After jotting down the contact details for the school, Allison said, "I think I may have some photographs of him somewhere. Would that help?"

"It would be brilliant if you could find them," Peter said.

"If I've still got them, they will be on my phone. It shouldn't take me too long to find them as I store them in separate albums." After scrolling for a while, Allison showed him a series of pictures. "This is the one I took the day I bumped into them in Berth."

Peter and Abbie studied the picture of a tanned, good-looking man with his arm draped over Emily's shoulder, while his distinctive, blue eyes stared confidently into the camera. They were sat at a wooden picnic bench, and in the background was a sign for The Willy Wicket pub. There was an unmistakable resemblance to Katie.

"Very handsome," Abbie said. "I can see why you suspect he might be Katie's father. What was he like?"

"Mostly okay. Well, except for one thing. I don't like to say, really. It might have been just a language barrier thing."

"Go on."

"He became annoyed if he thought anyone had touched his things. You know, he would go off on the deep end in the staff room if his things had been moved. Go on about how we should have more respect. And that day. The day I bumped into him with Emily. He didn't exactly do or say anything, but he was possessive. I was going to join them at their table for a drink, but I quickly received the vibe I wasn't wanted. He was acting like he wanted Emily all to him himself, so I left them to it. I believe something more may have come of the relationship, but like I said, he had to rush home a few months later, and Emily stayed with Susan. Emily denied keeping in contact with him, but I've always wondered if that was true."

CHAPTER TEN

The research centre at the university was busier than on Peter's first visit, with numerous students milling around in the corridor. Margaret Adegboyega's place in the office was taken by a young brunette in a lab coat who introduced herself as Liz Doherty. "Margaret rarely comes in on a Sunday morning. Tapping the clipboard on the desk in front of her, Liz said, "My job is done. I'm here to check on the wellbeing of the participants who slept here overnight." Laughing, she added, "And to make sure they actually get up and leave. I was just on my way to the canteen. Would you like to join me? You'll find most of the students in there making use of the free breakfast we provide as a thank you for their participation. It's probably the only meal some of them bother with."

Entering the canteen, their ears were assaulted by noisy chatter. Taking their coffees to one of the last free tables, Liz asked, "How can I help you with Susan? She's away on a sabbatical, as far as I'm aware."

"So, we understand. Do you know where she is or how we could contact her?" Peter asked, raising his voice to be heard over the lively buzz of the room.

Liz shook her head. "No, sorry. I don't really know her." Shrugging, she said, "I don't really know any of them, if I'm honest. She is friendlier than Margaret, although that's not difficult to achieve. Unlike Margaret, Susan will ask about how the students are getting along generally." Lowering her voice and her head, Liz said, "I did hear a rumour once."

"Yes?" Peter said, leaning forwards to better hear.

"It probably was just silly gossip. For all I know, the story was made up by Margaret because of the difference between the two women. But it has been said that Susan was disciplined in the past for being too friendly with the students."

"Do you know when this was?"

"No idea. Before my time. It may have been elsewhere, or like I said, it might not even be true."

Looking around the room as one rowdy group started to leave their table, Peter asked, "Would you mind if we spoke to some of the students?"

Liz put down her coffee cup and said, "You're speaking to one now. I do this for a bit of beer money, the same as the others. Don't worry, I'm in my final year as a medical student, so I would know how to deal with an emergency should one occur while I wait for the cavalry to arrive." Looking up at the clock, she said, "Do you mind if we leave things there. I want to get in a few hours sleep before my shift at the hospital."

As Liz left, Peter noticed the student who had burst in on them during their previous visit. She was sitting with three other girls but was looking over rather than joining in their conversation. Picking up his mug of lukewarm coffee, he said, "Let's mingle," and headed across to the student's table.

Placing his mug on the table, Peter said, "Pippa, isn't it? Do you mind if we join you?"

Indicating the two empty chairs at the end of the table, Pippa said, "You can, but none of us know where Susan is."

"Oh?" Peter looked questioning at the three other students who suddenly had the urge to drop their heads and forage through the contents of their backpacks.

"I asked around after seeing you, yesterday," Pippa said. "No one has any idea where she could be."

As Peter and Abbie sat at the table, the three students stood. The smallest of the trio said, "We're off to the library. Catch you later."

"Sure," Pippa replied. "Meet in the Union bar at seven?"

Watching the three students weave their way through the

tables, Peter said, "They seemed keen to return to their studies."

"You know how it is. No one likes speaking to the police. Why are you so keen on finding Susan, anyway?" Pippa asked. "What has she done?"

"Nothing as far as we know. A close friend of hers has died. We want to let her know."

Pippa examined Peter and Abbie before asking, "Murdered?" Not waiting for a response, she added, "Not the woman that was all over the news last night? The one found stabbed in her garden?"

Without giving an answer, Peter asked, "Do you have any ideas that might help us to track Susan down?"

"I would love to help, but I really don't."

"Could you suggest anyone who might be able to help?"

"Sorry, again. I only knew her from here."

"What was she like?"

"Pleasant. She was always very professional and seemed to know what she was doing."

"And friendly?" Receiving no response, Peter said, "It was just I heard there was some gossip about her being over-friendly in the past."

"Where did you hear that?" Pippa said, before blushing, when she realised that she hadn't looked surprised by the accusation.

"What do you know about it?"

"My coffee has gone cold." Starting to stand, Pippa said, "I should be on my way."

Abbie stood, semi-blocking Pippa's exit, and asked, "How about I get you a fresh drink?" Pippa sank back to her chair, and Abbie said, "Three fresh coffees on their way."

Once Abbie walked toward the counter, Peter leant across the table and asked, "What did you hear?"

Pippa's face flushed as she mumbled, "It's a false rumour. Don't waste your time on it."

Peter scratched his head, before replying, "You seem awfully sure about that."

Pippa turned even redder. "I like Susan. I would help you to find her if I could, but I can't."

"So why are you so sure the rumour about her is false?"

Pippa looked into the distance before dropping her gaze to the floor. Quietly, she said, "Because I started it." Looking up, she added, "Not on purpose. I repeated something I heard when I shouldn't have."

"Go on," Peter encouraged. "What did you hear?"

"It was sour grapes. I knew that. It was stupid of me to mention it. When I did, people chose to make more of it. Susan has always been kind to me. I would take it back if I could. I don't even know the full story. He would never tell me. I don't think he has ever told anyone."

"Slow down," Peter said. "Who are we talking about?"

"My eldest brother. He studied there. When he saw the sleep project was running here, he told me to stay well clear."

"But you signed up, anyway?"

"It's easy money. Far less demanding than a part-time job to help pay the bills. Susan has been professional throughout and no one has approached me about anything else, like he warned."

"Approached you about what?"

Pippa shook her head. "I'm not entirely sure it wasn't all in his imagination. Sometimes his memory is a little hazy, unlike his imagination."

"Here we are, three coffees," Abbie said, handing out the mugs and taking a seat. "I ordered large ones."

"Thanks," Peter said, taking a sip. "Who approached your brother, and what did they want him to do?"

"Not my brother. They approached his girlfriend at the time, who attended Berth with him. I don't know exactly what happened, other than they split up over it. The girlfriend dropped out from her course shortly after. That's all I know. My brother would never talk about it, but I remember he was livid at the time. He stayed in a foul mood for months afterwards."

"Could we have your brother's contact details?"

"Can we do it the other way around?" Pippa asked. "I will contact him today and persuade him to contact you?"

"And if you can't persuade him?"

"I'll have a think about it after I've spoken to him," Pippa replied.

"Okay. Give us your number, and I'll ring you later this evening. How about the girlfriend? Did she have a name?"

"Elaine. I can't remember her surname, but I think she had a disabled, younger brother she used to care for. I have no idea what happened to her afterwards."

CHAPTER ELEVEN

Melanie's neighbour appeared next to the car before Fiona had pulled up the hand brake. She exchanged a look with Humphries as the neighbour tapped on her window before they had released their seatbelts.

She was a slight woman of about fifty years old wearing a ripped pair of jeans and a baggy top. Eagerly looking towards the house while bouncing on the spot, she said, "Hi, are you the police? It was me that called this morning. I've been watching the house ever since, but there have been no signs of movement. I hope Melanie's okay. I heard all about her daughter. I'm struggling to comprehend how something so dreadful could have happened in our little village." Edging closer to the house and trying to peer in through the window, she asked, "Do you think it was the same person? What if she is lying dead on the floor in there? It doesn't bear thinking about."

The neighbour was far too excited about the prospect of becoming involved in a murder investigation in Fiona's opinion. Sometimes that proved useful, but more often it wasted time. They were too keen to say what they thought the police wanted to hear. Convinced they had seen things that fitted into their preconceived ideas. "You should return to your home now, Mrs …?

"Jessica, but everyone calls me Jess." Craning her neck to get a glimpse inside the house, she added, "It seems strange she's not up and about this time of the morning. She usually is."

Fiona moved around to block any farther approach to the house. "You can leave it to us now, Jess. We'll come to your house afterwards to speak to you."

Shaking her head, Jess asked, "What do you think happened? Is no one safe from being murdered in their beds these days? What is the world coming to?"

"Melanie is staying with her other daughter. It could simply be a burglar heard the house was empty and took a chance. The sooner you return to your home and let us get on, the quicker we'll know."

Finally, accepting she wouldn't be allowed to get a closer look, Jess took a step back. "I'll get the kettle on and leave the front door on the latch. Just walk right on in when you're ready to take my statement."

"Thank you. We'll be with you as soon as we can," Fiona said, thinking that was hardly the actions of someone who genuinely feared for their safety. Once Jess left, she led the way toward the house. After rattling the front door, Fiona said, "It seems secure. We'll check around the back."

The back door had been forced open and broken glass littered the doorstep. Sliding in through the partially open door without touching it, Fiona said, "We'll take a quick look around and then call it in."

The kitchen appeared neat and tidy. The only thing slightly out of place was one of the drawers was partially open. There was no way of knowing whether it had been left that way by Melanie. Looking around, Humphries said, "Thank goodness for nosey neighbours. From the front, there is no sign of a forced entry."

"She could talk the legs off a donkey, that's for sure. I'm hoping she got a good look at the intruder," Fiona replied.

An archway led into a large room that served as a dining area. The living room looked the same as it had the day before. Upstairs, the five doors leading from the landing were open. Fiona made a mental note to ask Melanie if she had left them that way. They peeked inside the four, double bedrooms and family bathroom. Nothing appeared to be damaged or disturbed in any way, but that didn't mean the drawers hadn't been searched and contents taken. They moved on up to the top floor, an open-plan area containing every child's toy Fiona imagined existed. Looking out over a massive garden that backed onto the rolling countryside, she called Melanie.

"Hi, Melanie Clifton? It's DI Fiona Williams. We spoke yesterday. I'm afraid I have some more bad news for you. Your back-door has been forced open," Fiona said, as she descended the stairs. "We are here now. As far as we can tell, nothing has been taken, but you will need to contact someone to repair the back door." Entering the kitchen, she added, "I can't see any signs of damage. All your electrical equipment seems to be undamaged and left in place. Could we drive over to speak to you and Tasha?" After receiving directions, Fiona said, "We should be with you in just over an hour. Can you make sure Tasha is available to talk to us?"

Once Fiona had returned her phone to her pocket, Humphries said, "Next door to see Miss Marple?"

"After you, Inspector Clouseau."

"Does that make you Cato?"

"For that, you can lead the interview with Jess, and I want you to wind it up within fifteen minutes," Fiona said. "I will time you."

◆ ◆ ◆

Fiona and Humphries left the house half an hour later, carrying a brown paper bag crammed full of homemade cakes but little new information. It had taken a while for Jess to admit she hadn't seen the person on Melanie's property. She had seen a figure walking down the lane in a suspicious manner. She couldn't clarify what struck her as so suspicious, but apparently, she could tell from the way they walked that the person wasn't a local. She was unable to give a description as the assumed intruder wore an overcoat with the hood pulled up.

"Interesting that Jess was so sure the intruder wasn't a local, and definitely not Susan," Fiona said, driving away. "That destroys any argument that Susan killed Emily and returned looking for their daughter."

Peering into the bag of goodies, Humphries said, "Could you identify your neighbours from the back if you saw them hurrying away?"

Fiona had a clear view from her bedroom window of five of her neighbours. She was confident she could recognise them from only a quick glance. "Yes, even though, unlike Jess, I'm not at home much."

"Really? With 100% accuracy?"

When Fiona thought about it again, she remained convinced she could pick out her adult neighbours, but she wasn't sure she could distinguish between the neighbours' children and their friends. Stubbornly, she replied, "Yes," despite the seeds of doubt creeping in.

Humphries contented himself with the cakes during the journey to Wick. Tasha's home, The Maltings, consisted of a stone cottage, a courtyard of tumbledown stone barns, a large garden full of self-seeding plants and three paddocks. Getting out of the car and stretching, Fiona's attention was drawn towards the paddocks. Shielding her eyes from the sun, she couldn't help smiling at the antics going on. She wondered if Emily's chicken run was a response to Katie's requests to visit her aunt Tasha more often.

One paddock contained a collection of chicken, geese and ducks mingling around a manmade pond, the second contained goats with an assortment of play equipment ranging from a trampoline to slides and see-saws. They also had an old boat and a ramp giving them access to the roof of their shed. The third field was occupied by miniature ponies who had a selection of traffic cones and large plastic balls to entertain them.

Fiona was about to push herself away from the paddock rails when Melanie appeared by her side and handed her a mug of coffee. "I was making myself a cup when I saw you arrive from the kitchen window." Glancing across at the two goats arguing over who should stand on the highest part of the shed roof, she said, "They're so funny. I could watch them for hours. Of course, Katie adores them."

"Where is Katie?"

"Inside doing a jigsaw puzzle with Tasha." Sighing and looking out across the paddocks, Melanie said, "It's such a crying shame my Tasha can't have children. Don't say I said anything, but all of this is nothing more than a substitute. She had no interest in animals as a child. Not even the family cat."

"We would like to talk to Tasha alone, but I won't mention a thing. Your secret is safe with me." Gazing out at the animals, Fiona asked, "Is it possible Emily kept in contact with Katie's father without anyone knowing?"

Melanie blew across her coffee, before saying, "Anything is possible, but I doubt it. She was either at work or with Susan and Katie. She could keep something like that a secret from me, but I can't see how she would have kept it from Susan. How is she, by the way?"

"We haven't managed to contact her. Other than the number you gave me, do you know of any other way we could get hold of her? Details of where her parents lived or places she liked to go?"

Creasing her forehead in thought, Melanie said, "I don't remember her talking about her family, other than saying her parents were dead. I'm Katie's only grandparent, you see. She has no one else to care for her."

Not wanting to be dragged into the custody of Katie issue, Fiona asked, "Did Susan ever mention where she grew up?"

"Now you mention it, I don't think she ever did. There was a slight northern twang to her accent occasionally, Manchester maybe. It wasn't marked, so she could have left there as a child."

"Why do you think she left Emily?"

"I haven't a clue. None whatsoever. One minute everything was hunky-dory. The next, she was gone."

Silence fell as the smaller goat won the argument on who should take the highest spot. The larger goat bounded down the ramp and started to head-butt another goat who had been happily minding his own business. Shaking her head at the antics, Fiona returned her attention to Melanie. "How are you doing?"

"Just about holding everything together. For Katie's sake, as much as anything. She's my little ray of hope. We've been discussing her education. I'm thinking of enrolling her at a private school rather than sending her back to the village school. I think it will hold too many reminders of Emily. A fresh start away from all the gossip and unpleasantness would do her a world of good."

Although she was no child expert, Fiona wasn't convinced uprooting Katie from everything she knew and removing reminders of her mother would be helpful in the long run. Especially as Melanie had argued previously that Katie staying in the village with her would be the least disruptive option. She made a mental note to check on what rights Susan would have if she appeared with a good excuse for her absence. Melanie's assumption that custody would pass automatically to her could be wrong.

"It's funny," Melanie continued. "I keep looking, but I see nothing of Emily in Katie. She's so angelic and perfect in every way. I was thinking last night that she is more mine than Emily's."

Concerned by how Melanie was comparing her daughter so unfavourably to her granddaughter, Fiona watched Melanie's facial expression as she tracked the defeated goat across the paddock. She sounded disappointed with her daughter. A strange emotion when she had just been brutally murdered. "How do you mean?"

"If you think about it, when Emily was born, she had the ovaries I created inside of her. So, you see, Emily was my mother's child, and Katie is mine."

Fiona didn't see it at all but was too taken aback to think of a reply. Her mind was busy questioning whether a mother would kill a daughter to take a grandchild for herself.

Pouring the rest of her coffee away, Melanie turned abruptly towards the house. "Shall we go in and find Tash and Katie?"

Fiona turned to follow, trying to make sense of Melanie's logic. She had temporarily forgotten about Humphries. He was sat on the bonnet of the car, sipping the coffee Melanie had brought out for him, staring at his phone screen. Walking towards him, she asked, "Has something new come in?"

Dawning on him that Fiona was talking about work, Humphries quickly logged out of Twitter and put his phone away. "I don't think so."

CHAPTER TWELVE

She rubbed her red, raw hands, irritating the cracked skin as she watched the two women chatting. Were they talking about her? How could they when they don't know anything? The only weak link to the plan is Jake. But he would never tell. He promised me, and I believe him. Even if he lied and told his mates, they would never willingly speak to the police. Boys of his age simply don't.

No one would ever suspect me of wrongdoing. I'm the sort of person that if you passed me in the street, you wouldn't notice I was there. If you did, you would smile back at me. I was always taught to smile. Never to frown or draw attention to myself.

People talking about me is rather alarming. I've always been such a quiet, non-descript type of person. Honest and good, although rather a daydreamer.

Children in Need made me cry again this year. I think I care too much. I've always wanted to help others.

They shouldn't have lied to me. They told me everything would work out fine. And like a fool, I believed them. They took what is rightfully mine.

I've so much love inside in me to give. It scares me when my heart feels like it will jump right out of my chest because it has so much love to give.

I never knew there could be so much blood. Or how it would stain my hands. I've scrubbed and scrubbed until my hands are raw. Two bars of soap, and still the blood remains. If only they hadn't been so foolishly stubborn. Only thinking to apologise when it was far too late. God is on my side. They were in the wrong.

Breathe. I must breathe deeply, and the dizzy spell will pass. They caused this anxiety. I hate them for making me so weak. So compliant. It is my turn to be strong and stand up to them.

Inside on a lovely day like this? When we settle into our little cottage by the sea, we will never waste sunny weather. On summer days, we will be outside exploring. On winter nights, we will snuggle around an open fire under cosy blankets. We will read books and tell scary stories. Well, not too frightening. Just a little scary. There will always be a happy ending. I will make sure of it.

CHAPTER THIRTEEN

Melanie held the front door open for Fiona and Humphries before leading the way to Tasha's kitchen. The room was cluttered with pots and pans, cookbooks, quirky paintings and an abundance of animal photographs. A double, old-style Aga dominated one wall. Above it hung a crucifix, and in front of it, two collies were curled up in a basket. Katie sat at a battered, scarred table. She was so engrossed in searching for jigsaw pieces for the half-completed puzzle showing a traditional farmyard, she didn't look up. Tasha stood at the open window, twisting a dishcloth in her hands with a faraway look on her face.

Tasha had similar features to her sister, but her face was makeup-free, and her mousy-blonde hair was tied back in a simple ponytail. Her hands were strong and calloused, with short nails devoid of polish. The faraway look in her eyes slipped away, and she gave a warm and welcoming smile. "Come in and sit down."

Fiona approached a chair covered in newspapers and Humphries one covered in folded blankets.

Moving toward the table, Tasha said, "Just plonk it over there, somewhere. Can I get you something to eat or drink?"

"We're fine, thank you," Fiona said, taking an interest in the puzzle. Picking up a piece, she handed it to Katie and said, "Try it there." When the piece fitted, she was rewarded with a wide grin.

Katie looked completely at home in the untidy kitchen with a tower of folded washing as her backdrop. If Katie could say where she wanted to live, Fiona thought she would say she wanted to stay here with her aunt.

Tasha took a seat next to Katie, smiling encouragingly at the puzzle's progress.

"We are sorry for your loss." When Tasha looked away, Fiona added, "Families can be complicated at times, can't they?"

Melanie hovered near the kitchen door, looking uncomfortable. "Would you like me and Katie to walk the dogs?"

Tasha nodded, and Katie climbed down from her chair without making any complaint. Fiona wondered if she was always so perfectly behaved or in a state of shock and operating on autopilot.

The dogs reacted enthusiastically as Katie pulled on a pair of pink wellingtons, and leads were collected from a hook by the kitchen door. When the back door clicked shut, a silence fell in the kitchen, breaking the spell of domestic bliss. Fiona took the opportunity to look around and spotted a leather-bound, well-thumbed bible on the side counter.

Focusing on the puzzle, Tasha said, "Mum has told you things were strained between me and my sister?" She continued when Fiona nodded, "I'm not sure how I feel at the moment. I've been remembering happier times. When we were children and then teenagers venturing out on our own for the first time. Us against the world. That is how I want to remember Emily. Not the difficulties of the last few years."

Tasha slotted a puzzle piece into place and stared blankly into space. Fiona and Humphries caught each other's eye as Tasha's mind appeared to drift elsewhere. The dreamy looked was replaced with one of exhaustion when Tasha finally spoke again, "I haven't cried yet. Is that terrible of me? I don't seem to be able to switch from being angry with Emily to mourning her. Do I sound uncaring and an absolute bitch?"

Gently, Fiona said, "People react to sudden loss in a variety of ways. Not being in floods of tears doesn't mean you're hurting any less."

"You're right," Tasha said with a start. "Dave doesn't understand, and mum is struggling enough as it is. It does hurt, but I would be a hypocrite if I broke down and cried. So, I carry on, trying to be the practical one. Do what people expect of me." Turning a puzzle piece over in her hand, Tasha said, "It's funny how that happens. Once your role in a family is established, it's set for life."

There was a low rumbling sound from outside. Tasha looked towards the window, and asked, "Was that a motorbike?"

"Sounded like it," Fiona said, thinking how isolated the spot must be to take notice of the rare sound of passing vehicles.

"Strange. We don't usually hear vehicles on the road from here unless there's a north wind." Turning her attention away from the window, Tasha said, "You don't want to hear my nonsense. What is it you want to know? Mum said there has been an intruder in her home. Was anything taken?"

"We're not sure, but it doesn't look like it."

"Maybe they were disturbed. The neighbour doesn't miss a thing. Mum said you wanted to speak to me."

"Yes, that's true," Fiona said, playing for time and trying to find the right words for her next line of questions. "There is no easy way to ask this, and I'm sorry if you find it upsetting."

"I much prefer plain speaking," Tasha said, returning her attention to the puzzle pieces spread across the table.

Fiona considered Tasha. On the outside, she appeared tough and resilient. The family mask could be hiding a fragility, but she had no option other than to plough on. "We understand you fell out with your sister when she became pregnant. It was shortly after you discovered you couldn't have children. Is that right?"

Tasha scanned the puzzle pieces as she said, "That's when our disagreement started. I was devastated at the news and hitting out at everyone. I said some unkind things about her behaviour and was judgemental about the fathering of Katie. In retaliation, she became critical of my marriage and lifestyle choices. She started a rumour that Dave was violent, which couldn't be further from the truth. She hated it when mum brought Katie over to visit. She would have stopped it completely if she hadn't relied on mum so much to babysit. Things escalated from there."

"Melanie is very generous with her time," Fiona said, still trying to grasp the logic of the comments she had made outside. "Was that always appreciated?"

"By me, yes. Emily was one of those people who never seemed satisfied."

"Did your mother and sister argue?"

Tasha shrugged. "Mum has complained that Emily made last-minute changes to her plans. I've no idea if they argued. You would have to ask her."

"How did you get along with Emily's partner, Susan?"

Slotting a puzzle piece into place, Tasha said, "I wasn't given the chance to get to know her. Emily told everyone that because of my religious beliefs, I was homophobic and wouldn't accept her relationship. That was also untrue, but people were happy to believe her. When we fell out, many decided that I had become bigoted since marrying Dave and joining the church."

"You're not at church this morning?"

"I take great comfort from the scriptures, but God isn't tied to a building. And anyway, we share our vicar with several other churches. We only have a service here in the village, once a month. Those I never miss. Occasionally, I attend mass at the other churches, but I can honour him just as well, right here."

"What caused your infertility?"

"Oh, I'm not infertile, and clearly, neither was Emily." Taking a deep breath, Tasha said, "I have a form of Canavan Disease. Mum prefers to skate over the subject because of the guilt of knowing she is a carrier. I only discovered the condition after several miscarriages. The likelihood of me having a healthy baby is low. There is a far higher chance of me giving birth to a child that will have a short and painful life. We decided the risk was too great to continue trying. I wasn't angry about Emily becoming pregnant. I was furious that she refused to take any tests to ensure she was carrying a healthy baby. The rift between us grew from there."

"So, Emily was lucky that Katie was born unaffected?"

"Extremely. I would be a liar if I said I felt no resentment at all, but I think we would have gotten past that in time, if it hadn't been for everything else."

"Everything else?" Fiona asked, wishing Tasha would lift her head from the puzzle so she could read her expressions.

"The hurtful allegations that I was homophobic and the constant criticism of my relationship with Dave. Things were hard enough with all the stress from the miscarriages. We didn't need that as well."

"Which fertility clinic were you referred to?"

"We decided not to go down that route. Once we had the result of the tests, we decided to accept we wouldn't have children. I know there is a small chance I could have a healthy baby, but I felt it was too much of a risk to take. The disease causes progressive brain atrophy and death before reaching the age of ten. Research is going on all the time, but currently, there is no cure or useful treatment. Would you knowingly risk exposing an innocent child to that future?"

"Probably not." Furrowing her brow, Fiona said, "So, your mother was fortunate as well as Emily?"

Tasha shrugged. "What can I say? The family luck ran out when it reached me." Hearing the engine of an approaching car, Tasha finally looked up from the puzzle. "That will be Dave, I expect."

The car engine grew louder and stopped, followed by the sound of a car door creaking open and slamming shut. "We're nearly finished," Fiona said as Tasha looked anxiously towards the door. "Does the name Dr Jeffrey or The Merrion Clinic mean anything to you?"

"Never heard of either of them." When the back door opened, Tasha called out, "Dave, have you ever heard of Dr Jeffrey or The Merrion Clinic?"

"A tall, stocky man with curly, dark hair and a full beard dressed in dust-covered jeans, a tatty sweatshirt and steel-toed work boots crossed the room to the sink. Washing his large, calloused hands under a stream of water, he said over his shoulder, "No. Why? Should they?"

"These are the detectives investigating Emily's murder," Tasha explained. "They wanted to know."

Dave flicked on the kettle and filled a mug with instant coffee before joining them at the table. Casting a concerned look over Tasha, he asked, "What is the connection between a clinic and Emily's murder?"

"We're not sure there is one. It was a long shot, to be honest." Looking across at Humphries, Fiona said, "I think we're finished here, so we'll leave you in peace. There is one thing before we go. You said there is research into the condition. Do you know where it is carried out?"

"Sorry. No idea. I've just heard mention there is some." Taking her husband's hand, Tasha said, "That sort of thing isn't for us. God decides our path, and we put our trust in him."

CHAPTER FOURTEEN

Driving out of the courtyard, Fiona and Humphries waved to Melanie and Katie, walking the dogs across an adjacent field. "Thanks for taking a back seat back there. What do you think?" Fiona asked.

"I thought the conversation was best left to you, but I'm wondering if Emily approached a clinic for tests despite what she told her family."

After waiting at the road junction for a powerful-looking motorbike to pass, Fiona said, "Me too, but I can't for the life of me understand why she kept it a secret, knowing her silence was creating an issue. Unless they had previously expressed everything should be left in God's hands, and she thought it might make things worse."

"I can't think of any other explanation," Humphries agreed. "So, the million-dollar question. Do you think Tasha's jealousy and resentment spilt over into violence?"

"A possibility worth bearing in mind, but my gut feeling is no. She seemed more resigned to the situation. She didn't fake tears and was honest about her range of emotions. I have more doubts about Melanie. She said some pretty weird things while you were waiting by the car about Katie being as much hers as her daughter's. She's adamant she will have custody of Katie."

"Would a mother harm her own daughter?" Humphries said, shaking his head as if to rid it of an unpalatable thought.

"Not normally, but something about Melanie feels off-kilter."

"They are providing each other with alibis," Humphries said. "But a premeditated attack on her daughter so she could take custody of Katie? I'm finding it hard to get my head around that."

"I know what you mean but we have to consider the possibility. And if we suspect her of that, then we have to consider whether she has harmed Susan Penrose."

"Nothing suspicious came out of the interviews of Emily neighbours. Surely, at least one of them would have noticed something odd about Melanie," Humphries replied.

Fiona sighed. She didn't like entertaining the idea any more than Humphries, but a detailed background check on the whole family was warranted. Directing her mind elsewhere, she said, "I wonder if Susan Penrose was ever involved in research into this Canavan disease. Had you ever heard of it before?"

"It's a new one on me," Humphries said, double-checking there were no cakes left in the bag.

"There's some homework for you, right there. See what you can learn about the disease and the ongoing research."

"You do realise it's a Sunday, don't you?"

"And?"

"You're getting as bad as Peter. Don't you ever switch off?" Avoiding the look Fiona was giving him, Humphries examined the bottom of the empty paper bag. Satisfied he had eaten every last crumb, he said, "Even if Susan was involved in the research, what difference would it make?"

"I don't know. I just have the feeling it is relevant somehow. Although Tasha denied knowing the Merrion clinic, that's where we're headed now. Can you ring ahead and check there will be someone there able to speak to us? We should arrive in an hour or so."

◆ ◆ ◆

The Merrion clinic was in a four-storey, Georgian house surrounded by a large, formal garden. Fiona and Humphries were surprised to be approached by two burly security guards as soon as they stepped outside the car. Despite showing their warrant cards, they weren't allowed into the building until they were searched, and the clinic confirmed they were expected.

The reception area managed to feel both sterile and plush. In a starched white uniform, the receptionist led them along a brightly lit corridor and up a spiral staircase before directing them into a waiting room. The highly polished floor and sumptuous leather armchairs were complemented by a large-screen television and a complicated-looking coffee machine.

"Carly will collect you from here when her appointment finishes. It shouldn't be too long. If you need anything, please let me know."

"I'm sure we'll be fine," Fiona reassured the receptionist.

While Humphries set to work operating the coffee machine, Fiona picked up the clinic's shiny brochure. A speedy flick through confirmed Carley was Carley Seller, the Clinic Administrator. The clinic was led by a consultant in reproductive medicine and a pioneer in reproductive genetics.

Fiona's attention was drawn to Andrew Thomson, the Laboratory Manager who had taught at and carried out research into cryopreservation at Manchester university. A quick Google search confirmed her assumption that cryopreservation was preserving organisms at sub-zero temperatures. She exchanged the brochure with Humphries for a cup of coffee. "Read the bit about Andrew Thomson and his previous work. He was in Manchester the same time as Susan was a student there."

While Humphries studied the brochure, Fiona's mind wandered to her personal situation. Had she left things too late? Would she end up somewhere like this if she wanted to start a family? Children had never factored into her plans. But then, neither had growing old alone. Many women waited until they were in their thirties to start a family, but she wasn't in a situation to be even thinking about the possibility in the near future. Her relationship with Stefan could never work long-term. Not without one of them making a major change, and she had no intention of being the one to change.

Would she be happy to content herself with being the dotty aunt to her brother's two children? They used to meet regularly at their parents' house before dad had the stroke, but since then she had hardly seen them. She had to call her sister-in-law last Christmas to discover what gifts she should buy. Previously, she had always known.

Carley strode into the room with her arm outstretched in greeting. She was a slim, attractive brunette in her early thirties. A conservative dresser, Fiona admired the way the woman carried off a bright orange, figure-hugging dress, a black blazer and killer heels while still looking professional.

"Hello, I'm the clinic administrator. I hope you haven't been waiting too long."

Standing to shake hands, Fiona replied, "Not at all. It's good of you to see us on a Sunday."

"I'm the first point of contact for many couples, and a Sunday is often easier for them. There's no one else here today, so we can talk in here or go back to my office?"

"Here is fine," Fiona said, retaking her seat. She watched Carly walk across the room like a model on a catwalk to close the door and make herself a coffee.

Over her shoulder, Carly said, "Do either of you want a fresh cup?"

"I could do with a refill," Humphries said.

Taking her seat, after handing Humphries a coffee, Carly asked, "As officers were you able to avoid the attentions of our new security?"

"No, they were very thorough," Fiona replied. "You said they were new?"

"We employed them after poor Dr Jeffrey's death. We have all been rather on edge since. We have received the odd letter in the past but nothing to suggest we were in any real danger. I struggle to comprehend how some peoples' minds work. In the past, I've considered the activists who accuse us of playing with God's plans as harmless nutters. We don't carry out abortions or experiment on animals, so I thought we were safe from attacks. Now, I feel vulnerable just driving into work every day."

"You've received threats before?" Fiona asked.

"Not personally and nothing recently. I think the last letter the clinic received was over a year ago. But you know all this surely? I thought you were here to update us on the enquiry."

"Sorry, we should have explained the situation when we rang. We are from a different station, investigating another murder that may be connected to Dr Jeffrey's."

"Another doctor?"

"No. A young mother. Emily Clifton."

"Good God! They've killed a client!" Carly said, putting her coffee to one side.

"You recognise the name?"

"No, sorry," Carly replied, blushing as she realised her mistake. "I just assumed the clinic was the connection. Is that the case?"

"We're not sure. Her family were under the impression she conceived her daughter naturally, but perhaps you could check and tell us whether she contacted you for tests?"

"We have strict confidentiality rules, so you will have to make a formal request. You said she claimed to have conceived her child without treatment. If that is the case, why do you think there is a connection to the clinic? We wouldn't normally run tests for a natural pregnancy."

"The tests would have been for Canavan Disease?"

"A GP could send those tests off to the labs just as easily as we could. Make an official request, by all means, but it is highly unlikely we would have been involved under those circumstances. Was there any other reason you thought there might be a connection?"

"The circumstances of her attack have clear similarities with Amanda Jeffrey's," Fiona said carefully. "How much do you know about it?"

"Nothing more than what has been reported in the newspapers. I understand she was stabbed to death in her kitchen, and her house was ransacked. The local police have discounted a disturbed robbery and think it was because of her connection to the clinic. Amanda had no enemies, so who else could it have been other than a fanatic with extreme views about our work?

Until that person is found, we are all afraid they could strike again. That's why we've upped security."

"Have you had any thoughts about why Dr Jeffrey was the chosen target? Why her and not say, the lead consultant?"

"That's the frightening thing. We've no idea why she was chosen. To think there's a stranger out there prepared to randomly kill any one of us because of the work we do is terrifying. I blame social media for the increase in such extreme beliefs. Don't they understand we help women here? We're helping to create life, not destroy it."

"It's hard to know why people think the way they do, although I do agree the internet has a lot to answer for. I understand Dr Jeffrey worked here on a part-time basis."

"Here, yes. Amanda was semi-retired and had more of an advisory role. She worked ten mornings a month. She didn't have her own client list. She transferred from our parent company on Harley Street, where in the early days, her research was high profile and considered to be cutting edge."

Making a mental note to speak to the parent company, Fiona asked, "How did you get along with her?"

"Okay, I guess. She was getting on in years and tended to keep herself to herself, but she was always very polite and pleasant."

"Do you know what she did with her remaining time? Was she connected to any other clinics in an advisory or a more active role?"

"That would be against company rules. I believe she was a keen gardener. Apart from that, I really can't tell you much about her private life."

Noticing Carly checking the time, Fiona said, "Sorry, are we keeping you from something?"

"No, nothing urgent. I will be going home as soon as we're finished here, and I'm sure our receptionist would like to get home to her family." Carly quickly added, "But discovering who murdered Dr Jeffrey is more important. Have you been told about the break-in that happened the week before the murder?"

Annoyed that she hadn't, Fiona replied, "We are in the preliminary stages of our investigation and only recently spotted the similarities in the two cases. What was taken?"

"As far as we could establish, nothing. It is possible they took copies of whatever documents they were after."

"Documents?"

"They targeted Amanda's office and forced open the cabinets containing patient's files. We checked everything against the computer records and found nothing had been physically removed."

"Was it a particular type of file they were after?" Fiona asked.

"It was hard to tell. All the drawers had been pulled out and left scattered across the floor. We wondered at first if they had been looking for drugs and became angry when they couldn't find any. That was before the murder, of course."

"How did Amanda react to the break-in?"

"Shocked. The same as the rest of us."

"Is it possible Amanda kept paper files on some patients that weren't backed up on the computer records?"

Carly shook her head. "Everything should be entered into the system."

"Maybe, she kept personal files for her own use along with the official files?" Fiona persisted.

Carly replied, "Anything pertinent to the client and their treatment would be logged onto the computer," but Fiona detected a hint of doubt in her voice.

Humphries looked up at the red, blinking light in the corner of the room. "Was anything picked up on the security cameras?"

"Those were put in after the break-in. Before then, we only had cameras trained on the front and rear entrances to the building. The limited footage we do have is with Silton station. There is an image of a slight person wearing an oversized hoody that no one recognised leaving the building at the right time. The footage was so fuzzy, and the person's face was concealed, so it hasn't proved to be much help."

"A slight person?" Fiona asked, thinking how the vague description matched that of the person seen leaving Melanie's home. "Did you have any impression whether it was a man or a woman?"

"If I had to say one way or the other, I would say female. But it was hard to tell anything."

Catching Carly looking at the clock again, Fiona said, "Just one more question for now. Does the name Dr Susan Penrose mean anything to you?"

With a blank expression, Carly shook her head. "Sorry, no."

CHAPTER FIFTEEN

Fiona rang Silton station to be told the officers handling the Dr Jeffrey murder investigation were unavailable until tomorrow morning. When she updated Peter, he said they should finish for the day and be in for a seven o'clock briefing the next morning.

Driving out of the clinic, Fiona said, "Your girlfriend is in luck. Peter said we can go straight home."

"Aha. You know why that is?"

"No idea."

"He's got a new lady friend. How he manages it, I don't know. A French widow, I believe. She moved into the village a few weeks ago, and he's *helping her to settle in.* Oh, la la."

Pushing against an irrational surge of jealousy, Fiona said, "His private life is none of my concern."

"Do I sense a hint of envy there?"

"Of course not. Don't be stupid," Fiona replied.

"Okay, I'm backing off quietly," Humphries said, holding up his hands in surrender. "You really need to get yourself a boyfriend. Or girlfriend. It's all the same to me. Have you tried using a dating app?"

"Humphries! Shut up!"

After dropping Humphries off at the station, Fiona had over an hour to kill before her meeting with Ben Creasy. She drove to the Boars Head pub where they had agreed to meet. She hoped that by the end of the meeting, she would have something solid enough to point Plymouth station in the direction of Eliot McCall and the previous investigation Dewhurst had signed off as closed.

The small, unlit car park at the rear of the pub had space for only a handful of cars. The exterior walls of the pub were covered in signs advertising upcoming football matches. She cringed when she saw the amount of broken glass, razor blades and straws scattered on the ground.

It wasn't the type of pub she fancied sitting in alone for too long, although she would prefer to arrive before Ben so she could choose where they sat. Checking the time, she considered calling Stefan before deciding against the idea. She would be home when she got home. Instead, reminded by the name, she opened the kindle app on her private phone and settled back to read the Ben Elton book she had downloaded weeks ago but had not had the time since to read.

She was lost in the storyline when her phone rang. Seeing the caller's name, she was tempted to ignore it. Her brother only rang to berate her for her failures as a daughter or because he desperately needed a favour. With ten minutes to go before her meeting, she would have rejected the call if it hadn't been for their father's poor health. There was always a slim chance it could be something important. Hitting accept, she said, "Hi. Is there a problem?"

"I'm afraid so. Something has cropped up, and we can't be there to collect mum and dad from bingo tonight."

Fiona's rising irritation collided with her sinking heart. She thought it was probably as dire an emergency as a chipped nail, or they had run out of wine, and she regretted answering the call. "Sorry, I can't help. I'm still at work."

"They don't need picking up for another hour or so. I'm sure they wouldn't mind waiting a few minutes."

How very considerate of them to be so patient. "I have no idea how late I might be. Why can't one of you collect them?"

"Long story. A problem has been brewing with the neighbours for a while, and it all kicked off this afternoon. It needs to be sorted tonight. Mum said she hadn't seen you for over a week when I dropped them off. You know how she misses you."

Fiona looked up to see Ben Creasy enter the pub. The guilt trip combined with no time to argue. Just perfect. "Tell them I will be there, but I might be a few minutes late."

"Can't you ring them?"

"No," Fiona said, ending the call and hurrying across the pub car park.

CHAPTER SIXTEEN

Ellie felt herself nodding off to sleep. She was exhausted and should have gone up to bed an hour ago, but she didn't want to disturb her daughter asleep on her lap.

Phone and radio reception was erratic in the area, and after automatically searching for a channel, her radio had selected one she had never heard of before, Smooth Country. It proved to be the only channel it would play, so she was being educated in music all the way from Nashville. One song called, *I Hope You Dance*, had resonated with her, and she started to sing the chorus as she gently rocked her daughter. "I hope when you have the chance to sit it out, you choose to dance."

She pulled the pink Little Princess nightdress over her daughter's chubby knees. She was perfection. From the top of her head to her cute, little toes. All present and correct. She recalled her younger days when she craved love from a partner. Not that she had ever been starved of love. She loved her parents and adored her brother and husband. But nothing came close to the overwhelming love she felt for her daughter. It welled up inside of her, threatening to burst her heart into a thousand pieces, it was so powerful. It chased all rational thought from her mind. Looking down at her daughter's twitching eyelids, she felt the fire of a tigress fighting to protect her cubs, deep inside her.

Looking up at the darkness of the night, she supposed her impossible hopes and fears for her daughter were shared by mothers around the world. She wanted her child to be loved and perpetually happy. To have the perfect life without misery, betrayal or tears. A fulfilling career, a caring husband and a circle of close friends. She wanted her to grow into an adult who always had a smile on her face and laughed readily, who cared for others less fortunate, and no matter how busy or successful, always found times to look up at the sky and wonder at the possibilities.

Sighing, she thought back over her own life. On the whole, life had been good to her. Her parents had given her the confidence to grab hold of opportunities with both hands. It was only recently that she opted to sit things out. It was time she set a good example for her daughter. She resolved to always choose to dance whenever there was an option.

CHAPTER SEVENTEEN

Fiona inched herself out of bed while Stefan was asleep. Feeling around for her clothes in the dark, she banged into the bedside cabinet, causing Stefan to stir.

"What time is it?"

"Early. Go back to sleep."

Fiona grabbed the last of her clothes and carried them from the room when Stefan groaned and rolled over. She had wanted to get into the station early in the hope of updating Peter on what Ben Creasy had told her. Unfortunately, she was already running later than she wanted to be.

In the bathroom, she splashed water on her face in the hope it would magically make up for her lack of sleep. While Peter considered Susan Penrose to be their main suspect, Fiona was increasingly concerned about her safety. Melanie's comment about her daughter's ovaries had repeated in her mind, keeping her awake most of the night. What if Melanie was responsible for murdering both women, possibly with Tasha's help, so she could get her hands on Katie?

Leaving the house, the early morning sun warmed her face and lifted her mood. It had been a long, dark winter with none of the usual things to look forward to due to the covid restrictions. The warmer weather was a much needed, welcome surprise.

Before heading into the station, she popped into the Squire Inn to pick up a coffee. The pub opening to serve breakfast was a sure sign that Birkbury was being dragged into the modern world even if it was going kicking and screaming. The pub providing the over-priced, extensive range of coffees, half of which she had never heard of, rather than an impersonal chain store, was its rural take on modernisation. Initially, Peter had been appalled at the development, but even he couldn't resist the delicious pastries they served. She tended to read the news online, but she grabbed a newspaper on her way to the counter.

She spotted several young men waiting to be processed through the station's front doors, so she headed back through the car park to the rear entrance. The bangs of locker doors in the corridor announced the night shifts were ending. After numerous greetings and one officer playfully trying to relieve her of her coffee, Fiona entered the empty operations room and sank onto her chair without removing her jacket. She stared into space and sipped from her coffee as her computer screen flickered into life. She jumped at the sound of heavy footsteps behind her, burning her mouth on too large a gulp of coffee.

Humphries plonked himself on an adjacent chair with a hearty, "Morning!"

Recovering herself, Fiona said, "You gave me a fright. What are you doing in so early? I thought you had a hot date last night."

"She got fed up with waiting."

"Sorry."

"No worries. With an empty evening, I did as you asked. Susan Penrose has never been involved in fertility research of any kind, let alone Canavan Disease. Her expertise is in sleep disturbance, and she has restricted her research to that area. There have been no unexplained breaks in her work records, where she might have been up to something else. She started her work at Berth Uni. She moved when the programme was transferred to Birstall."

"No breaks until now," Fiona corrected him. "I assume she still hasn't been in contact?"

"It seems that way," Humphries replied. "You don't think she is our main suspect, do you? You think she hasn't been in contact because something has happened to her."

"It concerns me she has changed her identity in the past, but she hasn't done anything as Susan Penrose to raise any suspicions. She hasn't even been caught speeding."

"She could have been doing anything under her real identity," Humphries said. "We have no idea why or how she was able to take up a dead girl's place at university. Maybe her application was turned down, and she can't handle rejection. Professional or personal."

"Maybe," Fiona replied, not sure if Humphries was making a serious point or not. It was often hard to tell with him. "I still think it's more likely something has happened to her than she attacked her ex-partner several months after they split up."

"You two wet the bed?" Peter asked, walking in carrying two cups of coffee and a paper bag with the pub's name emblazoned across it. He took out a pastry for himself before placing the spare coffee and bag on Fiona's desk. "I saw your car in the car park," he said by way of explanation. "Sorry, Humphries, I didn't see yours out there. How did you get in this morning?"

Humphries rubbed his generous stomach. "I cycled in. I'm watching my weight, aren't I."

"You're what?" Fiona spluttered, remembering the cakes he had scoffed the day before. "That's the first I've heard of it."

"Gotta keep in shape for the ladies, isn't that right, Peter?"

Peter ignored the comment and walked to the windowsill to take a seat. While he organised balancing his drink and pastry, Fiona broke her pastry and offered half of it to Humphries along with the fresh coffee.

"I'll make an exception," Humphries said, taking a bite.

"Abbie won't be in for an hour or so," Peter announced. "How did you two get on yesterday?"

Fiona related her odd conversation with Melanie and confirmed the rift between Emily and her sister. She went on to explain what they had learned at the fertility clinic and her concerns for Susan's safety.

After listening, Peter asked Humphries what his thoughts were.

Humphries finished his mouthful of pastry before saying, "I agree the family need investigating, and there may be a connection to the fertility clinic. For all we know, this drunken one-night stand may have never happened. The clinic may have been involved in the pregnancy itself."

Peter interrupted and said, "We have a possible lead on the identity of Katie's father. If it proves to be correct, the clinic's possible involvement would be limited to testing for this disease you mentioned, which the clinic said was unlikely."

"Canavan disease," Humphries said, looking pleased with himself.

Surprised, Fiona said, "We drew a complete blank asking her family who they thought Katie's father might be."

"So did we with the group of friends Emily shared with Susan, but we had more luck talking to an old college friend she kept in contact with. At about the right time, Emily was friendly with a German, exchange teacher called Carston." Peter pulled up the image of him and Emily in the pub garden on his phone and passed it to Fiona. "He does bear more than a passing resemblance to Katie."

"Definitely," Fiona said, wondering how Melanie would react to news of a father who could claim custody as she passed the phone onto Humphries. "Does he have a surname, and have you managed to track him down?"

"I'm going to leave that in the capable hands of Abbie when she arrives. She should be able to obtain his full name and last-contact details from the school that employed him. One of her many, hidden talents is she speaks fluent German. What did Silton station have to say about a possible connection?"

"I haven't spoken to them yet. Someone should be on duty after nine o'clock. Do you think Melanie, with or without the help of Tasha, could be responsible for murdering Emily? It wasn't only what Melanie said, it was the way she said it. The whole conversation made me uncomfortable. It was as though having custody of Katie more than made up for the loss of her daughter. She could be responsible for Susan's disappearance as well."

"Finding Susan Penrose remains our priority," Peter said, looking thoughtful. "What you say does tie in with what her friend

Allison said. She told us about an episode where Emily was convinced her mother was trying to steal Katie away from her. It was put down to postnatal depression causing a psychotic episode. A mother killing her daughter is a hard pill to swallow, but it needs a closer look, if only to eliminate the possibility. Any other theories?"

"If Susan had a professional connection to the Merrion clinic, she might have been the intended victim, not Emily," Fiona said. "Her hiding somewhere could explain why she hasn't come forward despite the appeals."

"Unless she's staying in a nunnery in the Himalayas, there's no way the news of Emily's death hasn't reached her," Humphries said. "Even if she is in the States for a job interview the news should have reached her by now."

"If she is, she didn't leave the country on a passport in the name of Susan Penrose," Peter said. "She's covered her tracks wherever she is. There hasn't been a single call from anyone claiming to have seen her. Even the usual crackpots have been quiet. According to a student on her sleep research programme, she may have been recruiting for a different type of trial in the past."

"What type of trial?" Fiona asked.

"I'm not sure. There's a girl called Elaine who might be able to fill in the details. I'm hoping to track her down today while Abbie is searching for Carston. Rachel and Eddie are heading to Oxford. We had some luck with the CCTV coverage of the train station. I've sent them rather than rely on local officers so they can follow up on anything interesting. We know that when Emily arrived, she took a taxi to Browns on Woodstock Road. They will be talking to the taxi driver and the restaurant staff. We might get lucky and discover who Emily met that day. Humphries, can you and Andrew concentrate on taking a closer look at the family?"

Turning to Fiona, he said, "If Emily conceived naturally, I can't see her having an obvious connection to the clinic, but it could be via Susan. She might be responsible for both murders."

Before Fiona could say anything, Humphries said, "I checked last night and this morning. Susan has never carried out any fertility research or been connected to the clinic in any way as far as I can see. Her work has always been closely related to sleep issues."

"She's still a scientist. I'm not sure how wide their circle is," Peter said. "It could be the connection is a more personal one. See what you can find, Fiona."

Fiona didn't argue with Peter's reasoning as it gave her an excuse to pursue her vague suspicions and see where they led. After taking a sip of her coffee, she nodded to Humphries, and said, "Our investigations may overlap. As they couldn't find another motive, Silton station have assumed Dr Jeffrey was killed because of her work by a religious fanatic. We only skated over the surface yesterday, but Tasha and her husband are religious and made it clear they were anti-medical intervention. The rift between the two sisters may have been started by the pregnancy, but it continued because of lifestyle differences."

"Who is the family liaison?" Peter asked.

"There was a mix-up with it being a Sunday, and Melanie relocating. Davina Box is due to meet them this morning," Fiona said.

"I've worked with her before, and she's good. Raise your concerns with her. If there's anything to uncover, she'll find it." Standing and stretching, Peter said, "Abbie should be in shortly. We'll meet back here at six o'clock. Fiona, can I have a quick word?"

CHAPTER EIGHTEEN

Once inside Peter's private office, he asked, "How did the meeting with Ben Creasy go?"

Fiona slumped into a chair. "The good or the bad news, first?"

"Go with the good. Then I can at least dream for a few minutes."

"Ben Creasy saw Eliot in his car the night the girl was killed. He is prepared to give a written statement saying that he was not in his bedroom studying as his mother claimed."

"And the bad news?"

"Oh, there's more. Ben rang the station at the time and gave this information to an officer involved in the case. He expected his call to be followed up by a request for a formal statement, but that never happened. Unfortunately, he has no idea who he spoke to on the phone. It could have been a simple oversight."

"I thought he was friendly with the convicted boy's father. Why didn't he come forward with this information when the lad was charged and tried for the murder?" Peter asked.

"That's the bad news. A couple of days after Ben called the station, his van with a few hundred pounds of cigarette and booze was picked up on a random search. He said it was a favour for a friend who was getting married, and it was all for the reception party. Funny enough, the officers didn't believe him. He was already kipping on a friend's couch after his wife kicked him out, so instead of sticking around for the investigation, he decided it was a good time to relocate. If he gives a statement, he wants that little incident forgotten about."

"Which isn't going to happen," Peter said. "Even if it did, this guy will have no credibility. A friend coming forward at this late stage with a vague recollection of talking to someone won't wash."

"I thought you would say that, but not all is lost. The reason he remembers seeing him that night was he watched him pull over to do a deal with Jason Gray."

"Who, as far as I can remember, is inside for dealing," Peter said.

"Out early for good behaviour."

Peter leaned back in his chair while drumming his fingers on the desk. He leant forward, and said, "You're wading into dangerous territory, talking not just overlooking evidence, but making sure it disappeared. Especially as your star witnesses are petty criminals. I think you should step away now and concentrate on Emily Clifton."

"While an innocent boy languishes in jail," Fiona protested.

"Hardly innocent. He had a long history in juvenile."

"While a privately educated friend of the right people is free to kill again. Will you be the one to break the news to the parents of the next girl that turns up strangled?" Fiona knew the comment was below the belt, but she could tell from Peter's face it had hit home. For good measure, she added, "Tell me you could look them in the eye and say the police are doing all they can to keep people safe."

"I understand what you are saying, but the fact remains we're looking at using the word of two, petty criminals against the word of a government minister and his family. Have you forgotten that we are living in a world where it is acceptable for a government minister to check his eyesight in the middle of a pandemic by driving his family hundreds of miles to a local beauty spot?"

"It was Eliot's mother who said he was at home," Fiona said, as she could see Peter's resolve weakening. "His father was conveniently elsewhere. My conscience won't allow me to say nothing, even if yours will."

"See if you can contact Gray and whether he is prepared to speak to us, but don't do anything else without speaking to me first. And I will be the one to tell Plymouth about Eliot McCall's involvement in a previous murder enquiry." As Fiona started to protest, Peter added, "And that's a direct order." He followed it up, by saying, "You obviously think something has happened to prevent Susan from coming forward."

"Yes, I do," Fiona replied stiffly.

"Run with it, but don't distract the others unless you have something concrete to back up your ideas."

CHAPTER NINETEEN

Bored of the computer game, Harry stared in the wing mirror, watching Katie's reflection. Not that there was much to see. She looked like a china doll sat so prim and proper. She was going to be a total bore. A day spent with Josh and Warwick was going to be bad enough. They were the geekiest kids in school. He would die of embarrassment if anyone saw them together. Trust his mother to fancy their father. Why couldn't she fancy a cool kid's dad? Anyone's dad would be better than theirs.

Tired of watching the sullen girl, Harry glanced across at his mother. Her face was all made up for a night out, not a walk around some dumb farm. The only good thing about the place was the adventure playground. He had been there before on a school trip. The teachers had deemed it too dangerous for them to go on the massive, killer slide and the zip wire. No one was going to stop him today with their silly rules.

At least he had been promoted to the front seat so the girls could get to know one another. He studied the view in the wing mirror again. The silence from the back seat suggested his sister, Becky, was equally as unimpressed with Katie. Becky was a bit of a brat, but she wasn't as bad as some little sisters. She could climb trees, play football and ride her bike as well as any boy. He couldn't see them having anything in common to talk about.

The one and only thing he would like to talk to Katie about was her mother's murder. Only it had been made quite clear to them before leaving the house that the subject was off-limits.

Looking back at his mother, he wondered what it was with the hair. He liked her curly, blonde hair, even if she constantly moaned it went frizzy. The cropped, dark hair made her look too different. Like she wasn't really their mum anymore but some strange impostor. Dad said it was a mid-life crisis thing. If only he knew the truth. This new haircut was for Josh's dad.

He had thought of telling dad about the friendship, but he was always away working and too busy to spend time with them. Maybe he had his own lady friend who coloured her hair and painted her nails for him. Grownups were weird.

If he told his dad, there would be months of grief. Two of his mates had been through a divorce. One thought it was great as his parents tried to outdo each other with the gifts they showered on him. The other said it was a right pain to discover the things you needed were always at the other parent's house. Overall, he liked things as they were. He didn't want to shift his belongings from house to house. Best to stay stum, but there was no way on earth he would be friends with Josh and Warwick. Nor was he going to babysit some orphaned kid who didn't speak unless she was spoken to. She just stared with those eerie, blue eyes. He would leave all that to his sister.

CHAPTER TWENTY

When Fiona contacted Silton station to talk about Dr Jeffrey's murder, they were over keen to share information and work together. It was evident that they had hit a dead end and were desperate for new leads and ideas. She had met the lead officer years earlier on a Domestic Violence course, and they had hit it off straight away, so she was happy to agree that a face-to-face meeting would bring them all up to speed much quicker.

Fiona met her in the reception and took her up what was laughingly referred to as the conference room. It was barely bigger than a standard interview room. The tables were the same, but at least the chairs had soft coverings.

Fiona had hoped to discover more about Dr Jeffrey's private life, but Silton had focussed all their efforts on extremist members of pro-life groups from early on in their investigation. She was disappointed to see how little time had been spent on Dr Jeffrey's recent activities. She couldn't help thinking that they had been too hasty to narrow down their investigation. "The partner is definitely out of the picture?"

"They had been together for years, and he was in Scotland visiting a sick relative when the attack took place. For what it is worth, in my opinion, his shock and grief are genuine. There was nothing to raise suspicions about him or her small circle of friends who were in the main, elderly academics or avid gardeners."

"Was her partner likely to gain financially from her death?" Fiona persisted.

"There's no financial motive. Their home is owned outright,

they have a pot of money from the sale of their London home, and he has a good pension. Dr Jeffrey received a generous allowance from a trust fund following the death of a wealthy relative. Those payments cease with her death."

"Did you run a check on past patients? People who may have been turned down for treatment or instances where things have gone wrong?" Fiona asked.

"She hasn't had her own patient list for years. She advised behind the scenes. Although her name is on the company literature, couples would not have met her. We did carry out all the usual investigations and came up with nothing. That's why we concluded the attack was related to the general work of the clinic, and she was chosen as an easy target. Here's a summary of our investigation. In the main, these extremist groups attacks are against doctors performing abortions, but there is increasing antagonism towards IVF clinics."

Reading the reports, Fiona was drawn to the biblical quotes the groups used in their criticism of fertility clinics. Her mind constantly returned to Tasha's parting words to her. "Our victim's sister is anti-medical intervention and is religious. We have nothing to suggest her beliefs are this strong, but the liaison officer will be teasing out her views." Raising her head, she added, "Officers are working on that angle, and I will keep you updated on any progress. I'm keeping an open mind. The family dynamics are strange, but someone killing their sister over religious beliefs? Despite her disagreement with our victim, she seemed very fond of her niece."

"Who will be granted custody of the child?"

"The grandmother thinks it should be her." Pushing back from the desk, Fiona said, "We will find out if any of the family are involved in any of these groups. Initially, I thought our victim may have used the clinic's services, but her family claims her child was conceived naturally, and we now have a possible lead on her child's father."

"If that's the case, why do you think the cases are linked?"

Fiona handed over a folder of their crime scene photographs.

"Similarities in the nature of the attack, the knife used and discarded at the scene and the damage done to the house." She went on to explain the hereditary disease, Canavan and the implications for a child conceived naturally. "Have you come across the name Dr Susan Penrose during your investigation?"

"It doesn't ring any bells, but I will double-check that name with my colleagues when I get back to the station. Talking of which, I had better be on my way."

Escorting her from the building, Fiona wasn't sure the meeting had been of much help to either side, and she had nagging concerns about the gaps in their investigation.

CHAPTER TWENTY-ONE

Despite her doubts, Fiona decided to start her own research into local, pro-life activity. Her concentration was disrupted by Humphries clicking the top of his pen while staring into space. She walked over to the whiteboard. Her attention was constantly drawn to the photograph of the egg found near Emily's body. Over her shoulder, she said, "What does an egg symbolise to you?"

"You're not still obsessed with that blasted thing, are you?" Humphries asked, without turning around.

"Humour me, okay. What does the image of an egg make you think of?"

"That would depend," Humphries replied. "Fried I would think of bacon but boiled I would think of toasted soldiers."

Unimpressed with the flippant reply, Fiona turned away from the board. An egg to her meant rebirth and new beginnings. She was convinced Emily's murder was somehow related to the fertility clinic and Dr Jeffrey's murder. She shook her head in despair at Humphries still clicking his pen and staring into space.

"What are you doing, anyway?" Fiona asked. "Other than daydreaming, that is. Have you found anything on the family?"

"So far, they are all coming up squeaky clean. Andrew has gone to speak to a couple of their friends, but I doubt he will come back with anything. Come and have a look at this."

Fiona peered over his shoulder at a grainy picture of a middle-aged couple with a teenage girl she assumed was their daughter. The blurred photograph was taken from a newspaper article. "What am I looking at?"

Tapping the screen, Humphries said, "These are the parents of the real Catherine Susan Penrose." Pointing to the girl between them, he said, "This was Catherine's best friend, India Jennings. She was in the car at the time of the accident but escaped unscathed. Afterwards, she was 'a great support to the parents,' even helping them with the funeral arrangements and the boring paperwork." Tapping the screen again, he said, "Take a close look. Do you think this girl could be our Dr Susan Penrose?"

Fiona leaned forward, peering at the screen. "Hard to tell, but she could be. See if you can find out where she is now."

They were interrupted by a PC bursting into the room. "Sorry to interrupt, but Susan Penrose's car has just come up on the system. It was left overnight in a Tesco's car park in Wheatley."

"That's on the outskirts of Oxford. I'll let Rachel and Eddie know," Fiona said, reaching for her phone. After speaking to Rachel, she was too distracted to return to her research. Susan being in the Oxford area was too much of a coincidence. The question was, did Emily meet her because they were getting back together, to discuss their separation terms or something completely different. Maybe she had been mistaken about Susan's innocence. They argued and things turned ugly because they couldn't reach an agreement on whatever they were discussing. But if that was the case, why had her car been abandoned?

Fiona closed her search of pro-life activists and wandered to the canteen for a coffee break, taking the newspaper with her. Flicking through the pages as she sipped her coffee, an article about an abducted child caught her attention. The child looked exactly like Katie. Everything from the halo of curls to the shape of her face to the way she stared defiantly into the camera. The family lived in Foxley, only a couple of miles north of their area.

Fiona read the report through several times, her eyes constantly returning to the photograph. The girl had been left in the garden playing with her dolls, while her nanny popped inside to make them a snack for lunch. When she returned to the garden the child was gone. The father owned a string of outside clothing shops and was a local councillor for the Conservative party. The mother worked part-time in a charity shop. Both claimed their daughter would not have left the garden by herself. There was nothing to connect the abduction of this child to Emily's murder other than the uncanny physical resemblance to her daughter.

She returned to her desk to concentrate on her work, but her mind constantly wandered to the newspaper article. She was about to call Foxley station when Peter and Abbie appeared. Abbie went straight to a desk while Peter came over to ask for an update.

"Silton station weren't much help. I'm looking at local activists in our area," Fiona said. "As far as we can tell, Tasha and her husband have never been involved with any of them. Humphries has spoken by phone to their friends, and Andrew is interviewing a couple of the more promising ones."

"Where is Humphries?"

"He is following up on something else," Fiona replied. "We might have Susan's real identity. We'll know more when he gets back."

"Great. Knowing who she really is will be helpful. I'm putting out another appeal tonight for anyone who has seen Susan to come forward."

"Her car has been found abandoned on the outskirts of Oxford. I contacted Rachel to let them know. The car being dumped suggests something has happened to her."

Their attention was diverted when Abbie's phone rang at the far end of the room. Crossing her fingers, she said, "Hopefully, this is the call I've been waiting for."

"Has anything been heard from the family liaison officer?" Peter asked.

"Humphries spoke to her earlier. She's still getting a feel for the family dynamics," Fiona replied, as their attention turned to Abbie's phone call.

Not speaking German, Fiona had no idea what was being said

and could tell little from Abbie's tone and body language. As the call dragged on, Humphries came in and quietly said, "I might be onto something. India Jennings disappeared at the same time Susan Penrose took up her university position."

"Did anyone report her disappearance?" Peter asked.

"She was an only child. Her parents died shortly after her seventeenth birthday. Between then and the car accident, she had virtually moved in with the Penrose family. She would have had easy access to everything that would have made it possible for her to take over her friend's identity and her university place."

"Do you know the current whereabouts of the family?"

"Both parents have since died due to natural causes."

Abbie ended her call and announced, "We now have a full name, Carston Bocker. He has been teaching over here during the last few months at a secondary school in Plymouth. Annoyingly, his flight back to Germany is just taking off. Sorry, if I had been a few minutes quicker, we might have been able to stop him at the airport. Local police are going to talk to him as soon as he lands."

"Well, that's something at least. Plymouth is only a couple of hours drive away," Peter said. "Shame he wasn't teaching in Oxford."

"He may have been there. His contract with the school was only for the Easter term. I'm checking what he's been doing since then," Abbie said, her fingers already flying over her keyboard.

"If he's not involved in the murder, then it's one hell of a coincidence he was in the country at the right time. Post-Brexit, I don't know what the protocol is now," Peter said. "I guess I'll have to speak to Dewhurst. Did the officers you've been speaking with seem quite happy to assist us?"

"Once I got through to the right people, I didn't sense any reluctance. My guess is, if he doesn't agree to assist us voluntarily, it's likely to get more complicated."

"He seems to enjoy it over here, although he might not be quite so keen on prison food," Peter said dryly. "I'll try to catch Dewhurst before he leaves. I suggest we call it a day. We should have a better idea in the morning after we've heard from our colleagues in Germany and Rachel and Eddie have reported back from Oxford, which way we're going with this. After speaking to him upstairs, I'm going to have a quick beer in the Squire if anyone wants to join me."

Preparing to leave for the pub, Fiona's head was spinning with the quick succession of events. Discovering Susan and possibly Katie's father had been in Oxford at the time of Emily's visit suggested all manner of possible explosive situations. Had they all met up? What could they have discussed other than Katie? And how had that led to Emily's murder?

CHAPTER TWENTY-TWO

Like many pubs, during the Covid pandemic, the Squire Inn had revamped their outside area. Peter generally still chose to sit inside but made an exception for the Squire. The landlord had built a fully stocked, outside bar with the beer pumps linked directly to the cellar situated conveniently under the rear of the pub building. Every time he came in, he insisted it was the best pint of beer he ever tasted due to the short distance it had to travel.

Due to childminding issues, prior engagements, and Abbie wanting to remain alert for when the German authorities called, only Fiona, Humphries and Peter met up at the outside bar. After one drink, Humphries made his apologies and left. While Peter was ordering a second round of drinks, Fiona checked her phone and realised it was still switched off from earlier. Three missed calls came up. Two from Stefan and one from her mother. She was debating slipping to the toilets to call Stefan back when Peter handed her a glass of wine. "Shall we sit over there?"

Fiona followed him to the empty table on the edge of the terrace. While she wanted to see Stefan, she hadn't spent much time with Peter recently, and she always enjoyed his company. They also had a lot to discuss. She wanted to know what was happening about Eliot McCall, and talk through the possible reasons for Susan, Emily and Carston meeting up in Oxford. She was also intrigued by the French widow Humphries had mentioned. She was repeatedly told she never switched off from work, so she decided to start with the latter. Slipping her phone back into her pocket, she casually said, "I understand you have a new neighbour."

Peter stalled his reply by taking a drink from his pint. "I wondered how long it would take Humphries to start rumours. He bumped into us in the Horseshoe the other night. It's about time he settled down with that girl of his. He's becoming quite the gossip."

"I think I ruined their plans for last night."

"I'm sure he'll survive," Peter said.

"So, who is she? The new neighbour."

"Simply that. She moved in a couple of weeks ago and is still finding her feet and getting to know the area. How are things with you? We've not done this for a while."

Before Fiona could reply, Peter's phone rang. Checking the screen before answering, he said, "It's Abbie."

Fiona was thinking of calling Stefan before she saw the colour draining from Peter's face. He was saying little, but it was clear something bad had happened. She wondered if the bad news was case related, they had missed Carston at the airport maybe or whether it was something personal. Peter's sons from his second marriage were at an adventurous age, and his daughter from his first marriage had a history of depression and eating disorders. She could tell from Peter's manner that whatever it was, it was something serious.

Ending the call, Peter said, "Katie has been abducted."

"What?" Fiona said, her mind shooting to the newspaper report of the other little girl, recalling every detail in full technicolour. "How? Where from?"

"A friend of Tasha's took her to Cattle Country with her own children. One minute Katie was there. The next, she was gone. The friend claims she took her eyes off her for a second while talking to another parent. When their conversation ended, Katie had disappeared. Abbie is checking with the airline whether Carston is travelling alone. She'll update us on what happens when he lands. Meanwhile, we're heading over to Tasha's house."

Grabbing her bag and rushing after Peter, Fiona asked, "How

long ago was Katie taken? Would there have been enough time for Carston to grab her before his flight?"

"It would have been tight, but possible," Peter said, starting to jog back to the station where his car was parked. "The friend wasted time looking for Katie. When she couldn't find her, she asked the park staff to search before it crossed her mind to contact the local police. By the time they arrived on the scene, she was hysterical and not making a great deal of sense. They assumed it was her child that had gone missing, leading to a further delay in contacting Tasha and Melanie."

Catching her breath after jumping in the passenger seat, "Do we have the exact time for when Katie was last seen, and the time Carston's flight took off?"

"Carston flew out on a pre-booked flight from Exeter three hours after Katie was last seen."

"Okay, so it is possible he took her," Fiona said. "Cattle Country is about a twenty-minute drive from the airport straight down the motorway, but if he's travelling alone, where is she?"

"Abbie is looking at all flight details between here and Germany. He might not have been working alone. Melanie has confirmed Katie had a passport. We're checking whether it's still in the house. The friend is still with Tasha, so we can show her Carston's photograph. See if she recognises him or remembers anyone else who seemed to be loitering nearby. We can show her a picture of Susan at the same time."

Fiona mulled the situation over as the hedgerows flashed past. The resemblance of the girl snatched in the newspaper article dominated her thoughts. She pulled out her phone to search for the online reports of the abduction from the garden in Foxley. When she found one, the two girls' similarities were even more striking in the photograph used. After reading the report, she called the station. "A child called Amber Rice was snatched last week from her garden in Foxley. Could you find out the name of the senior officer handling the case and text through their details? Brilliant. Thanks."

"What's that about?" Peter asked.

"I happened to read the news report this morning. It may be nothing, but the girl snatched from Foxley could be Katie's identical twin. It's a long shot, but I want to make sure there is no connection between the two families."

Peter gave her a quizzical look. "Are you suggesting Katie had a twin? And now Carston, as the father, wants to take them back to Germany?"

"I don't know. I hadn't organised my thoughts that far, but I guess it's a possibility. The two girls are more than similar. They are virtually identical."

"If Katie was a twin, then only one of the mothers carried them. Emily's family and friends watched her pregnancy progress, so I guess it was her."

"Not necessarily," Fiona replied. "There have been cases where women have faked their bump."

"In the movies, maybe, but really?" After some thought, Peter said, "She might have been able to fool family and friends, but not her partner." His voice faded away when he added, "Who has disappeared off the scene."

Fiona rubbed her forehead in frustration. "If Susan was in on the charade from the start, why disappear now? Unless she's been silenced because she threatened to expose the truth."

"To who? Who would care that Katie was a twin?" Peter said, shaking his head. "Even if we don't hear anything from her after tonight's appeal, I'm hoping somebody who has seen her recently will come forward." After concentrating on overtaking a slow-moving car, Peter said, "We can't ignore the coincidence of Carston being in the country, but Susan's disappearance still concerns me. She brought Katie up with Emily as a couple, so it would be reasonable for her to want custody. Melanie clearly thought it was a strong possibility."

Fiona stubbornly disagreed. "Breakups can be messy, but they rarely end in murder. Not ones without any history of conflict. Susan killing Emily and then snatching Katie doesn't fit right with me."

"You've never met her," Peter said. "It never ceases to amaze me what people will do given the right circumstances."

"You still get a feel for people from the friends and things they leave behind. I think something happened to her."

"Emily told her family and friends that Susan had left her. Are you suggesting she was lying?" Peter asked, exasperation edging his tone. "Why would she do that unless she killed her?"

"If Emily killed Susan, then who killed Emily and snatched Katie? That doesn't make any sense," Fiona said crossly. Before she could say anything else, her phone rang.

Fiona's tone instantly changed to detached professional. "Thank you for contacting me. We're dealing with a child abduction which may be connected to Amber Rice's disappearance … The child has just been taken, so we're in the very early stages, but could you answer a couple of questions that might help us? … Could you ask the parents if the names Emily Clifton, Dr Susan Penrose or Dr Amanda Jeffrey mean anything to them? … The newspaper report didn't mention any siblings. Was Amber Rice an only child, and I know it sounds a bit irrelevant and callous, but do you know if the parents had any problems conceiving or whether she was adopted? … Oh, okay. If you could get back to me as soon as possible, we might have a link between the cases … Yes, as soon as I know more on this end, I will let you know …."

"Well?"

"He hung up before telling me anything useful."

"Did you catch his name?"

"Yes. DCI John Hillier."

"That figures. I've had run-ins with him before. Not the easiest of people to deal with. Everyone who knows him desperately wants him to take early retirement, but he doggedly keeps hanging on in there." Peter pulled over to the side. Flicking on his hazard warning lights, he said, "Show me this picture of the other girl."

While Peter looked at the photograph and skim-read the online report, Fiona said, "We know from the article Amber Rice was an only child. What if Dr Jeffrey was involved in the twin's conception, and the search through her office was to discover where the children were? Emily was murdered because she wouldn't say where Katie was that day."

Rolling his eyes, Peter handed back Fiona's phone, and said, "Let's not get carried away until there is a confirmed link between any of this." Indicating to pull out from the layby, he added, "I will try to set up a meeting with Hillier, but he will likely be uncooperative. If he proves to be difficult, I will go above his head. Him being so universally disliked may work in our favour."

Fiona's phone rang again. Seeing it was her mother calling, she was about to reject the call when Peter asked, "Aren't you going to answer it?"

"It's my mother," Fiona replied.

"So?"

Fiona hit the accept button. Before her mother could say anything, she said, "Sorry, Mum. I'm busy with work. Can I call you back?"

Ignoring the request, her mother said, "I've been trying to get hold of you all day. The boiler stopped working. Your friend Stefan very kindly came out and sorted everything for us."

"Sorry, what?"

"What a lovely man. He stopped and had a beer with your father afterwards. He has been trying to get hold of you as well. Can you ring him? He's worried about you. He says you work too hard. Well, I could have told him that. So will you ring him?"

"Look, Mum. Sorry. I really am busy. I'm pleased your boiler is sorted, but I've got to go."

"But what about your young man? You need to ring him."

"He's not my ... Sorry. I've got to go. As you're all such good friends, can you ring him and say I will contact him later."

As Fiona shoved her phone back into her pocket, Peter kept his eyes focussed on the road, his face unreadable as they lapsed into silence. Fiona was seething with anger. What the hell did Stefan think he was doing involving himself with her parents' domestic problems? She would kill him when she finally arrived home.

CHAPTER TWENTY-TWO

Susan Penrose reached for the bottle of water on the cabinet to the side of the bed. The plastic chilled her hand and the back of her throat as she gulped the water down in the hope it would stop her head from throbbing. It hurt so bad she couldn't think straight. She had no idea where she was or how she had arrived.

The last clear memory she had was of her standing in the cottage kitchen. Forcing her thoughts through the blinding pain, she visualised herself opening the fridge door to discover she was out of milk. The village shop would be closed. She would have to do without or drive to the supermarket a few miles away. Knowing there was no way she could cope without coffee in the morning, she snatched up her car keys that were in the small, wicker basket on the counter. No matter how hard she tried to remember, everything was blank after that.

The black hole in her memory lasted from her picking up the car keys until the first time she woke in the strange bedroom feeling sick and disorientated. She couldn't recollect how many times she had stirred and fallen back into oblivion, or on which occasion she had first realised she was chained to the bed.

She had no idea why she was here or who her captor was. Other than being drugged, she hadn't been harmed in any way as far as she could tell. Placing the plastic bottle on the bedside cabinet, she realised for it to be chilled, it would have been put there recently. She tried to remember if it had been there the other times she had woken, but the throbbing in her head prevented her from concentrating.

She examined the chains running from the cuffs on her wrists to the metal bedframe behind her head. Looking around the room, she registered for the first time that there was no window. She was in a decent-sized room in what she guessed was a cellar with one wooden door at the far end. The double bed mattress was comfortable, and the duvet cover and sheets smelt new, and they still had the crease from where they had been folded in the display packet. The floor was carpeted, and the room was heated to a pleasant temperature by two radiators. There was a small, wooden table with two chairs and an exercise bike in the room's far corner. Next to the bed, there was the cabinet and on the other side, a reclining armchair. Everything she could see looked brand new.

At the foot of her bed stood a commode. Her eyes filled as she recalled helping her mother on and off her commode in the final days before the pain and morphine left her bedridden. Little did she know back then, they were to be her last days as part of a loving family. Before cancer carried her mum away and her father decided he couldn't carry on without her. Not even to care for his daughter. Susan angrily wiped the tears from her face. This wasn't the time for maudlin over the past.

Judging by the length of the chains, she could reach the table and bicycle but not the door. She looked down at the chains and back at the door. She couldn't sit here and not at least try. After swinging her legs over the side of the bed, bright pinpricks of light danced in her vision. She placed her hands over her mouth, convinced she was about to vomit as the room slowly spun. She stayed in that position until her nausea receded. Looking down, she estimated ten steps to the door.

Taking a deep breath, she lowered her feet to the carpet and slowly stood. She staggered to the bedside cabinet, gripping the side and leaning over it to stop herself from falling. She waited while a hot flush washed over her to be replaced by a sudden chill. She straightened and with her arms out to her side to help her maintain her balance, she took a step towards the door. And another. Eight steps in all. A hollow laugh escaped. Her estimate had been wrong. There were another four steps to reach the door, but the chains prevented her from taking another step. Before her manic laughter turned to tears, she cautiously made her way back to the bed. Exhausted, she collapsed on the soft mattress and pulled the covers over herself.

CHAPTER TWENTY-THREE

As Peter and Fiona pulled into the gravelled courtyard of The Maltings, the front door flew open, and Melanie rushed out of the farmhouse, closely followed by a young woman with spikey, dark hair. Peter was unclipping his seatbelt when Melanie wrenched open the car door. "Have you found her?"

Climbing out of the car, Peter said, "Everything that can be done to find her is being done." He looked past Melanie to the young woman behind her, who looked equally anxious. "Are you the friend who took Katie out for the day?"

Guilt filled the young woman's face, and she looked like she was about to burst into tears. "Yes, I'm Sally. I swear I only took my eyes off her for a second. I don't know how this could have happened. Everyone knows how careful I am. Especially around strangers. It wasn't my fault."

Leaning over the top of the car, Fiona said, "No one is blaming you, Sally. Shall we go inside? We have a few questions that will help us to find Katie."

Sniffing, Sally said, "Yes, of course. I'll do anything that might help. I didn't do anything wrong, but if something happens to her, I will blame myself for the rest of my life. Please find her and bring her home safely." Sally started to shake and hyperventilate.

Fearing Sally was about to have an anxiety attack, Fiona took a firm grip of her arm. "Come on. Let's get inside so we can talk."

Melanie grabbed hold of Peter's sleeve. "Please find my baby.

She must be terrified."

"We're doing everything we can."

Crossing the courtyard, Fiona asked Sally if her children were inside. In clipped tones, Sally replied, "My husband collected them." Waving her arm in front of her, she added, "He thought it better they were away from all this."

Fiona registered the abrupt switch from fretfulness to bitterness. Catching Peter's eye, she knew he had noticed it too.

As they approached the front door, through her sobbing, Melanie starting mumbling, "We're coming for you, darling. Granny is going to find you and bring you back. She won't let anything bad happen to you."

Inside, Tasha and her husband, Dave sat at the kitchen table with their hands clasped together. The liaison officer stood to one side as Melanie took the seat next to her daughter and started to rock forwards and backwards as she continued mumbling or perhaps praying to herself.

"Is there another room we can use to talk to Sally?" Fiona asked.

Tasha raised her eyes to her liaison officer, "They can use the living room."

Peter took a seat opposite Melanie at the table as the liaison officer led Fiona and Sally through a short corridor to an austere living room. As they entered, goose pimples raised on Fiona's arms as the temperature dropped several degrees. It felt more like descending into a damp, cold cave than walking into a family room. The small windows created more shadows than light. A motley collection of chairs crouched around a large coffee table facing the fireplace. A radio sat on a side cabinet to the side of the fireplace. A small, unplugged television sat on a cabinet at the back of the room. The remaining wall was dominated by an intimidating, life-size painting of the crucifixion.

Sally took a chair close to the unlit fireplace. She nervously perched on the edge, twisting to face the back of the room, her eyes fixed on the blank television screen. Fiona took the chair next to her, registering it felt far less comfortable than it looked. The room appeared to be for earnest discussion and prayer rather than relaxation. From the doorway, the liaison officer asked if they wanted a drink.

"Unless you can conjure up a stiff whiskey, I'll give it a miss," Sally replied.

Fiona dismissed the officer with a slight shake of her head and a smile. She appreciated Sally probably meant it as a joke, but she detected a hint of derision in her tone. Although her eye makeup was smeared, Sally was a caricature of the yummy mummy. The type who carefully dressed for the school run, convinced how she looked outside the school gates and who she spoke to, was far more critical than the education that went on inside the building. She wondered how her friendship with Tasha had come about, as on the surface, they were polar opposites. Trying to put Sally at ease, Fiona said, "Maybe there's a den they use for relaxing."

"Afraid not," Sally said. "What you see is what you get."

Surprised by her knowledge of the house, Fiona asked, "Do you visit Tasha regularly?"

Sally jumped up to fully close the door before retaking her seat. Waving her bangled arm around, she said, "All this. It's Dave. Tasha just goes along with it to please him." With a look of mock horror, she added, "She occasionally does this thing called fun."

"What classes as fun?" Fiona asked, indicating Sally should return to her chair.

"I haven't managed to lead her that far astray," Sally said, with a snort of laughter. She immediately covered her mouth with both hands. "Sorry. Did that sound heartless? It's because I'm upset." Retaking her seat and looking anxiously towards the door, she asked, "Do you think they heard?"

Considering the thick stone walls, and the dark, fusty corridor they had walked along, Fiona said, "I doubt it. How do you and Tasha usually spend your time together?"

"We share a coffee from time to time. When I can get her away from this ... *Little House on the Prairie,* we do normal stuff like chat and shop."

"How did you meet Tasha? I hope you don't mind me saying,

but you seem quite different."

"Not really. We're both actresses playing a part." Running a hand through her artfully tousled hair, Sally said, "Sorry, I'm being overdramatic. I live on the ever-so-perfect, exclusive, housing development over the way. My daughter is obsessed with animals. She wants to be a vet when she grows up. Little sod kept sneaking over here uninvited. Tasha spotted her one afternoon and walked her home. I expected her to be furious. Instead, she said she was welcome to come over whenever she wanted to if that was okay with me. Our friendship has grown from there. She's a good person is Tasha. She cares. I guess that's why she's happy to go along with all the religious trappings. Isn't it all supposed to be about charity and good works? Well, that's Tasha all over. Not that any of her goodness has rubbed off on me. I just like the excuse to escape from my pristine life for a while."

"As her friend, has Tasha told you about what happened to her sister, Emily?"

"Yes, I came over as soon as I heard. Absolutely dreadful," Sally said, giving a theatrical shudder. "She's been so good to my daughter I wanted to repay her kindness. That's why I offered to take little Katie out for a fun day with my lot. I thought I was being helpful." Reverting to her whiny voice, Sally asked, "How could I have known this would happen?"

Fiona thought back over recent events. Should they have known? If she had raised her concerns over the physical similarities with the girl abducted from Foxley, could this have been avoided? The two girls must be connected somehow. A sudden thought occurred to her. "I don't suppose you know the date of Katie's birthday?"

"Sorry. You'll have to ask Tasha."

Pushing her feelings of guilt to the back of her mind, Fiona cleared her throat and asked, "Did she talk to you about her falling out with her sister?"

"She was upset by her sister's attitude. I have never met her, but I've heard all about her. She sounded pretty tunnel-visioned and small-minded to me. Which is strange when you think about it.

I hate people who demand their individuality is respected while denying the same right to someone else if their views differed."

"Has Tasha ever said she would like to harm her sister?"

"Oh, no! nothing like that. You have to understand that Tasha is the kindest, gentlest person you could ever meet. She doesn't judge people. Not like some. She viewed their falling-out as more of a failure. She said that once upon a time, they were close. If it wasn't for him, I think they may have called a truce."

Although it was obvious who Sally was referring to, for clarity, Fiona interrupted, "Who do you mean by 'him'?"

"Dave, her husband, of course," Sally replied. It was unclear whether the look of disdain she gave was aimed at the husband or Fiona's question. "To be fair, his main objection was Emily had hurt Tash, and he wanted to protect her. They are an odd couple, but he's as devoted to her as the other way around. Just he has funny ideas about everything else."

"Does he approve of your friendship?"

"He disapproves of the way I am, but he's not tried to stop us being friends. Their relationship is hard to explain. I don't dislike him, but I do dislike his holier-than-thou attitude. If I wanted life advice, I wouldn't seek it from an ignorant brickie."

"Nice place for a builder," Fiona said. While the house had a dreary feel to it, even if they had bought it in a half-derelict state and Dave had done the structural work himself, the location and land would have made it pricey.

"I thought the same thing," Sally said. "Melanie bought the place for them. I don't think Dave is a gold digger, if that's what you are thinking. I think he genuinely cares for Tasha. He just has odd ideas about everything else."

Fiona reassessed her first impression of Sally. Although she clearly disliked Dave, she was careful not to criticise him too much. She wondered if there was an ulterior motive for her going to such great lengths to provide a balanced opinion of him. Leaning forward, she asked, "How well do you know him?"

"I don't," Sally admitted. "I'm only going on what Tasha has said about him. I tend to visit when he's not around. If I mistime my visit, we exchange a cursory greeting, but that's it."

"You said earlier he disapproves of you?"

"Did I? Well, it's surprising how much you can pick up from a brief encounter, isn't it? As a detective, you must know how much can be conveyed in a quick hello."

Not wanting to push Sally into becoming more defensive, Fiona decided to drop that line of questioning, but it was something to consider later. "Did Tasha ever talk about her decision not to have a family?"

"You mean the inherited gene thing? It does sound grim. Tasha said it was a mutual decision on medical grounds."

"Do you believe it was by mutual agreement?"

"She's had every opportunity to tell me different."

Whatever faults Sally had, she appeared to be a fiercely loyal friend. Fiona wondered if she secretly envied Tasha's marriage. She was certain she would blindly defend her friend if she raised the possibility that Tasha might have an involvement in her sister's murder and the abduction. "Tell me about today at the park. Start at the beginning. When did you decide to make the trip and ask Katie along?"

"It was a last-minute thing. It was a lovely morning. My kids were driving me mad inside the house, saying they were bored. Once I decided to go, I thought Katie might like to come along. I hoped spending some time with other children would take her mind off things."

"Did Tasha not want to come with you? It was a beautiful day, like you said. It would have been a good opportunity for you two to have some fun together."

Sally's face turned crimson and she looked away. If she ever played poker, it would cost her a fortune. "I think she was busy when I called. She wanted to spend some time with her mother. Yes, that's it. Some good, old mother-daughter bonding."

"And the real reason you didn't invite her?" Fiona asked, catching Sally's eye.

"Okay, okay. You're right. Tasha would have liked to join us only I said my mother-in-law was coming along, and I thought it best it was just the two of us."

"Except it wasn't your mother-in-law, was it?"

"Will this all have to come out? I mean, I don't see what difference it makes."

"It will make a difference to how distracted you were. Plus, we need to interview your friend as well. The parent who momentarily distracted you."

"Yes, of course. How silly of me. He's just a friend. Another parent. We sometimes chat outside school. Our children are great friends, and it has thrown us together somewhat. As soon as I asked my two if they would like to invite a friend, they shouted at the top of their lungs for Josh and Warwick. Both parents work shifts. Either of them could have answered the phone when I rang. By chance, it happened to be their father, but that wasn't a foregone conclusion. I was offering to take his children off his hands for a while, but he insisted on coming along."

Fiona was aware she was being told a pack of lies, but the fact Sally resorted to babbling when lying was helpful. "I'm not interested in your friendship. What I need to know is how long were the children out of your sight? Was it truly only for a brief moment?" Pressing the point home, Fiona added, "Establishing the correct time-line is crucial to us finding Katie."

Sally fiddled with her hair before saying, "We told them to stay together. We had already walked around the park as a group to see all the animals. We saved the play area to last. We watched them for a while and then said we would go and buy them all an ice cream. We chatted for a bit and then went to the kiosk. The queue was longer than we expected."

"So roughly how long were they unsupervised?"

"We were always nearby. They were only out of our sight for a short time," Sally said defensively.

"How long?"

"Maybe half an hour or so."

Fiona thought it likely the children were out of her sight and mind for quite a while longer, and they were doing more than chatting, but accepting the time given, she asked, "Did the children see anything?"

Sally shook her head. "When we left, they were playing nicely together. When we returned, we discovered they had split up, and Katie had somehow become lost between the two groups."

Fiona slipped photographs of Carston Boker and Susan Penrose from her file. "Did you see either of these people hanging around the park?"

After studying them, Sally said, "I can't be sure. The warm weather had brought out the crowds, but I don't think so."

Taking the photographs, Fiona said, "I will need to speak to the other parent and all the children involved."

"An officer has already spoken to them. They didn't see anything. They didn't even realise Katie was missing until after we returned."

"I will still need to see them and show them the photographs. It might jog a memory of something they didn't think was relevant at the time."

"Sure. I understand, but not now surely. They'll be asleep."

Fiona looked at the window, surprised to see the room reflected in the inky blackness of night.

"Are you finished with me?"

"For now, yes." Handing over a card, Fiona said, "If you think of anything else that might help us, please ring me."

CHAPTER TWENTY-FOUR

Driving away, Fiona pulled out her laptop. "That's my twin theory out the window. The girl abducted from Foxley is nearly four months older than Katie. It is just about feasible that Carston fathered them both if he was a quick mover."

"An ongoing affair with Amber Rice's mother could have been the reason he applied for a teaching job over here," Peter said. "The liaison officer confirmed that Tasha and Melanie haven't left the house all day, and the husband has been working on a building site with five other men."

"That doesn't mean they couldn't have arranged for someone else to take Katie," Fiona pointed out.

"Why would they do that when Katie was already under their roof?"

Fiona shrugged. "Maybe Dave wasn't so keen to have his mother-in-law and niece invading his space."

"Anything to back that idea up?"

"No, not really. They're a difficult couple to read. I've no idea what they feel about Melanie and Katie staying with them."

"I didn't pick up on any antagonism. The liaison officer said she would stake her reputation on their shocked reactions being genuine when they were told Katie was missing," Peter said. "What did Sally have to say for herself?"

"She admits the children were left unsupervised in the play area for half an hour. My feeling is it was for much longer. I have the address for the other parent. Sally's children are currently at home with their father. They've already been questioned and claim to have seen nothing. I'll interview them and the friend tomorrow."

"Was the friend male by any chance?"

Fiona arched an eyebrow and said, "The friendship blossomed at the school gates while waiting for their children to be released."

"So, the day out was merely a cover, and it's unlikely they were fully concentrating on what the children were up to or what was going on around them. I'll arrange for photographs of Susan and Carston to be shown to the staff at Cattle Country."

They fell into silence, giving Fiona time to slip out her phone and switch it back on. Several text messages popped up. They told the story of how Stefan had booked and cancelled a table at The Manor Hotel, one of the most expensive restaurants in the area. There was no mention of his visit to mend her parents' boiler. She put her phone away, feeling a mixture of irritation and guilt but mostly tiredness.

CHAPTER TWENTY-FIVE

The temperature in the room was unbearable. The open windows sucked in heat rather than provide ventilation, but it was preferable to the wall of stale heated air that had greeted them when they first filed in. Sweat trickled down Fiona's side as her damp shirt limply clung to her back as she gave her update. Interviewing the members of the group on the day trip had been time-consuming and draining. The father was more concerned about keeping his affair a secret from his wife, than the disappearance of Katie. Like Susan, he was either oblivious or chose to ignore that their children hated each other. The children were equally indifferent to Katie's plight and blamed one another for not looking after her. Either way, they had all failed to have seen anything useful, and there was nothing to suggest they were responsible for the abduction other than by inattention.

It had been a long, unproductive day for everyone. No one had seen Katie disappear into thin air. Only it wasn't thin air. The crowded play area was situated alongside a busy car park. Katie had probably been bundled into a waiting car before Sally had selected the ice cream flavours. Fiona's mouth dried at the thought as she tried to find a comfortable position in her chair.

Carston Boker had purchased one flight ticket and flown home alone. His partner of several years had been waiting for him in Frankfurt. He had no criminal record and once his memory had been jogged, he had happily confirmed briefly knowing Emily Clifton. Once he heard a child gone missing, he voluntarily agreed to speak to them, and Abbie was currently on her way to the airport.

Fiona rolled her bottle of water across her forehead. The chilled plastic giving some respite from the heat. Next to her, Humphries was acting like a radiator. She shifted her chair away from him, trying to not make it look obvious. She felt hemmed in by Andrew and Eddie sitting directly behind her. She could feel their hot breath on her neck as the whole room seemed to pulsate with tension. She drank from her bottle of water, fighting the urge to pour the water over her head.

Peter paced in front of the whiteboard. "Until we hear from Abbie, I want our full focus on finding Dr Susan Penrose. Despite the violent death of her ex-partner and numerous appeals, she has failed to come forward. We have CCTV footage of Emily leaving the Browns restaurant in Oxford with a woman with spiked, dark hair. We are trying to enhance the quality to be sure, but the features, height and build match Susan's. Her car has been found abandoned in a supermarket car park. We are still trying to find an address for where she was staying. Why has she changed her appearance, and is someone shielding her?"

In a tired and weary voice, Fiona said, louder than she planned, "Or has something happened to her."

Without missing a beat, Peter continued, "We can't ignore the possibility something has happened to prevent her coming forward, but bear in mind there was no attempt to hide the two other murder victims' bodies. Susan has changed her hair colour and style, and she took elaborate steps to hide her tracks after leaving Emily. Someone, somewhere knows where she is."

"Her killer," Fiona muttered to herself.

"Are we definitely linking Emily's murder to the Dr Jeffrey case?" Rachel asked.

"For now, that remains a possibility. Has a link been found between Susan and Dr Jeffrey?"

"Nothing definite," Humphries said. "They were at Manchester University at the same time, but there is nothing to suggest they crossed paths."

Peter attached a picture of Amber Rice to the board. "Some of you may have seen the newspaper report about the abduction of this little girl from her garden in Foxley. The physical similarities to Katie are startling. Tomorrow morning Fiona is going to meet with the officers handling that case."

"If there's a connection, we need a bigger team to handle a murder and two abductions," Humphries said.

"My thoughts exactly. If there is a connection, I will request the two investigations are combined."

The suggestion made sense, but it was the first Fiona had heard of it. There was clearly some bad history between Peter and the Foxley lead officer. She wondered if she had been dumped in the middle of an age-old feud. From what he had said yesterday, she guessed he would be insisting the case came under his control rather than a shared responsibility. Peter didn't usually play politics, but there was an exception to every rule.

"That's it for today," Peter announced. "You all look exhausted. Go home and get some rest. Seven o'clock briefing tomorrow morning for everyone except Fiona. By then, we should have heard how Abbie's interview of Carston went."

Fiona rang ahead to tell Stefan she was on her way home and did he want her to pick anything up on the way. He sounded pleased on the phone, but she wasn't convinced she had been forgiven for the previous night's lack of communication as she collapsed into bed. When she explained a child had been abducted, he said he understood her priorities. She didn't think she was overthinking his comment about priorities. His English had improved, and he had grasped the subtleties of the language, so it wasn't a barrier or an excuse for misunderstanding anymore. There had been an unspoken expectation that she should rethink her priorities.

A headache started to form behind her eyes as she approached home. Her home. Her sanctuary from the ugliness she experienced at work. Her colleagues had relationships without being expected to change their priorities. Andrew had a young wife and child, while Eddie enjoyed a long stream of different girlfriends. She blocked out the voice of reason that told her that wasn't true for everyone. Peter had two marriages destroyed in different ways by the job, Humphries was always complaining his social life was being curtailed, and recently, Abbie's knowledge of a case had been used by someone she cared about. Her headache was threatening to turn into a migraine by the time she parked her car and inserted her key in the front door.

The door fell open, and Fiona was engulfed in a comforting, richly scented hug. She dropped her bag at her feet and clung to the warmth of the contact, wishing she could stay there forever and forget about everything else. That nothing mattered except here and now. Feeling safe and loved.

Stefan released her and gave her a wide smile. The one that turned her stomach to mush and her legs to jelly. The one that fogged her brain and made her think she could make this relationship work.

"I am so happy to see you home at an early time. We can have an evening like a normal couple, no?"

Fiona picked up her bag and headed towards the kitchen, wondering if her life could ever be described as normal. More to the point, what did Stefan think was normal? Was it her waiting by the kitchen sink for him to arrive home? That was something that never was going to happen. In the cheeriest voice she could muster, she said, "Hopefully, yes. Once I've had a coffee and changed, we can decide what to do." She crossed her fingers that a shot of caffeine would alleviate her weariness.

"What do you want to do? I could try to book The Manor again. They might not be too cross with me cancelling last night."

Fiona closed her eyes and reached for the headache tablets in the overhead cabinet. Opening them and pouring a cold glass of water, she said, "I've said I'm sorry." She added to herself, 'I didn't even know the table had been booked,' before swallowing the tablet with the water.

"Are you not feeling good? Work should not be so exhausting you are in pain."

"I'm good. A little tired is all." Turning to face Stefan, Fiona said, "I'll feel better after a shower. It will wake me up. What do you want to do? You decide."

"As you are so tired, why don't you have a long soak. I will collect a takeaway, and we can snuggle up on the sofa with an old movie. How does that sound?"

Relieved she wouldn't have to force her tired mind into making a decision, Fiona replied, "That sounds perfect." Maybe if she relaxed in front of the television, inspiration on the case might come to her. Every time she thought about the case, the faces of two, frightened, little girls filled her mind, while the creepy face drawn on that damn egg danced around the periphery.

"What would you like? Chinese, Pizza, Indian …?

Fiona's headache throbbed. Couldn't he decide for once? "I don't mind. Whatever."

"Chinese?"

"Yes, that's fine. The one in Sapperton is surprisingly good. There's a menu in the drawer, or there is one online."

"What would you like?"

"Anything. Honestly. Whatever you choose will be okay. I like all of it."

"That's not true. You do not like the fish dishes."

"Anything except fish."

"You like the seaweed dish, though?"

"Yes. Just get a selection," Fiona said, feeling like screaming. She left the room and headed upstairs before he could ask any more questions. Left to her own devices, she would be happy with a sandwich and an early night.

Stefan called up the stairs. "Take as long as you like. I will surprise you."

CHAPTER TWENTY-SIX

After a long soak and dressed in casual clothes, Fiona returned downstairs to wait for Stefan. Taking the warmed plates from the oven, she asked, "Do you want to eat at the table or in front of the television."

"Let's eat at the table so we can spread the dishes out."

Fiona laid out mats and cutlery. In her head, she ran through the conversation she wanted, no needed, to have with Stefan. Even if he wouldn't say where he had been the last month, she needed to set some ground rules for the future. Deep down, she knew the relationship couldn't work, but she wanted to hang onto the hope that if changes were made, possibly it could. Additional pressure from her parents was the last thing she needed. Once everything was ready, she called Stefan from where he was lounging in the living room in front of the television. Once he sat, she said, "Dig in."

Stefan raised an eyebrow. "Another of your strange phrases to learn."

Spooning food onto her plate, Fiona asked, "What have you been up to today?"

"I visited my uncle. He is very busy. He wants me to think about working for him."

Without looking up, Fiona said, "I take it from your tone you're not interested."

"I said I could help a little, but like you, I'm not in a position to commit to anything."

"What do you mean by that?" Fiona asked, aiming for a neutral tone but missing the mark. She focussed her attention on the food, waiting for his reply.

In between mouthfuls, Stefan said, "If Peter rang now, you would suddenly not be tired and grabbing your coat and shoes. Am I not right?"

Keeping her voice light, despite the irritation she felt, Fiona said, "If it was a work emergency and I was needed, I would have to go. That's not unusual in a demanding job." After a pause, she asked, "So what is stopping you from committing to helping your uncle? You haven't said where you've been recently."

"I've been up north. A girl thought she recognised my sister from a picture. I had to follow it up."

"Oh? Why didn't you say? You just left."

"I left a note. These people they don't hang around. If I hadn't gone straight away, I may never have found her."

Instead of commenting on the vague note, that had said nothing more than, 'I will be busy for a few days,' Fiona asked, "And did you find her?"

Stefan nodded before raising his fork to his mouth. After chewing, he said, "This is good."

Fiona tried to read Stefan's expression, but his head was bent over his food as he was shovelling it in. Was that to avoid the inevitable question she didn't want to ask? She mentally prepared herself for the answer, before asking, "Did she know your sister?"

Stefan stopped eating, putting down his cutlery and rested his hands on the table. The silence ticked by, hollowing out Fiona's insides. Dread rushed in to fill the void. Her appetite was gone as the pounding pain behind her eyes returned. Hesitantly, she reached across the table to place her hand over his. She squeezed it, willing him to look up.

Without raising his head, Stefan said, "She was there, but she moved on before I arrived." He pulled his hand away and picked up his cutlery to push the food around his plate.

"Hesitantly, wondering where there was, trying not to think

the worst, Fiona asked, "How was she when this woman knew her?"

"She was still fighting, but not good. She was weaning herself off drugs, hiding them so she could keep a clear head and get away. She disappeared one night. The girl thinks she escaped on her own terms. Only, she promised to make contact when she was free and come back for her. We waited, but nothing was heard. Then the girl. She, too, is gone."

Trying to sound upbeat, Fiona said, "Maybe your sister did escape and came back for her friend. She knows you are looking for her. Maybe they are trying to get back to you. Did you tell this other girl where you would be?"

"Right here. I gave this address, but it has been several days since I last spoke to the girl. I don't think they are coming."

Torn between sympathy and anger at her home being used, Fiona said, "Give it time." Battling with her conflicting emotions, Fiona said, "I wish you had told me sooner."

"I was waiting for the right time."

Fiona looked over the table at the rapidly cooling food still piled on their plates. "Have you finished eating?"

"Sorry, my hunger is gone."

"Mine too. I'll clear this away, and we'll go through to the other room to talk. Properly talk."

"I'll help."

"No, go and choose some music to put on or a film we can ignore in the background."

Fiona took her time separating the food that could be saved in the fridge. Throwing the last of the food in the bin, she heard Lewis Capaldi playing in the living room. She poured two glasses of wine and carried them into the room. Stefan was curled up on one end of the sofa, looking at the screen on his phone. She was about to comment when her phone rang. She handed one glass to Stefan and rested hers on top of the television. Reading her phone screen, she said, "It's Peter, I need to take it," before wandering back into the kitchen.

"Hi, Peter. Can I call you back in a minute?"

"It will only take a minute, and you're going to want to hear this."

"Have they found Katie?"

"No, but I've heard from Abbie. Carston could be her father, and we've got a definite connection between him and Dr Jeffrey."

Pulling out a kitchen chair to sit, Fiona said, "What? How could he be Katie's father? Sorry, that sounded dumb. So, they did have a relationship?"

"Not in the way we thought. He met Susan as well."

"I'm in the middle of something, and I'm too tired for games. What on earth do you mean by that?"

"In blunt terms, Carston was a popular sperm donor, paid handsomely for his efforts by Dr Jeffrey."

"I'm confused. What are you saying? Is he saying the three of them met up and Emily asked for his sperm? Is that how it works?"

Fiona didn't hear Peter's reply over the sound of the front door slamming shut. "Hang on a minute," she said, as she walked through to the empty living room. She looked out the window, just in time to see Stefan disappear into the darkness. Cursing under her breath, she asked Peter to repeat what he had just said.

"I know it's late, but do you want to come over? We could thrash out ideas on what this connection could mean. It could mean he fathered the Foxley girl in the same way."

Fiona picked up the glass of wine she had left on the side. An evening in Peter's snug cottage talking through the case sounded better than the tense conversation she needed to have with Stefan. Taking a sip of wine, it hit her how much Stefan had used her. Had he only appeared back in her life because he had given her address to some woman up north who was probably using a false name? And like a desperate fool, she had welcomed him with open arms. Battled with the impossibility of them having a real relationship. Tempting though it was, she told herself she should wait for Stefan to explain himself. "Umm, I had better not. I've had a drink. I'll give it some thought, and we can discuss ideas after I've spoken to Foxley station."

CHAPTER TWENTY-SEVEN

Fiona dragged herself out of bed when the alarm clock went off. She had finished the bottle of wine before giving up on waiting for Stefan to return. The click of the front door and his footsteps climbing the stairs had semi-woken her in the early hours. She had feigned sleep when the bedroom door opened, and he softly asked if she was awake. She felt childish when the bedroom door closed, and he slipped away. She must have gone straight back to sleep as she had no idea if he had spent the night in another room or had left the house. A part of her was too numb and weary to care.

The morning traffic was heavy, and it was taking ages to find somewhere near Foxley police station to park her car. As time was running short, she gave up her search and headed to the over-priced public car park that served the town's small shopping mall. Firmly putting thoughts about her disastrous private life to the back of her mind, she concentrated on how she planned to present her case to DCI Hillier as she hurried along the streets. Typical of most mid-sized towns, she passed several, closed-down stores.

At the foot of the steps to the station, she smoothed down her jacket and made her way to the main reception. She pulled out her warrant card at the desk and said, "I'm here to see DCI John Hillier. He is expecting me."

The desk sergeant looked her up and down before saying, "He left the building about half an hour ago. I'll see if he left instructions with anyone."

After waiting for ten minutes, Fiona was about to return to the desk when a dark-haired man dressed casually in jeans and trainers approached her.

"DI Williams?" he said, holding out his hand. "I'm DI Steve Dowell. I'm on the team working the Amber Rice case."

The firm handshake and dazzling smile failed to alleviate her irritation. "My DCI arranged an appointment with DCI Hillier."

"I'm afraid you will have to make do with me. I think you'll find that's an upgrade." Maintaining his wide grin showing a set of perfectly straight white teeth, Steve gestured with his hand. "There's a pleasant coffee shop along the way. I'm buying."

The coffee shop was tucked away on a cobbled side street. The walls were wood panels worn smooth with time, and the smell of coffee was overwhelming in the cramped area. Steve led her across the stone floor to a high-backed bench at the rear of the shop. Her coffee arrived in an oversized mug, with a heart marked in the froth. After taking a sip, she conceded it managed to be both strong and smooth. Just the way she liked it.

"I told you it was good, didn't I," Steve said. After drinking some of his coffee, he said, "Here is as private as anywhere. The message I received was that you are handling a case that might be connected to the Amber Rice abduction. What can you tell me about it?"

Fiona looked back through the shop at the constant queue of people waiting for coffees to take away. The few people sitting in for their drinks gravitated towards the benches at the front of the shop overlooking the cobbled street. She took another sip of the excellent coffee and launched into her summary of the two murders and Katie's abduction. DI Dowell, call me Steve, asked intelligent questions throughout her spiel and occasionally made notes. The few times she looked up, he appeared to be listening intently, and despite her mood, she found herself warming to him.

When she came to an end and fell silent, Steve looked back through his notes which she noticed were written in the correct shorthand. He leaned back in his chair, tapping his pen on the edge of the table. "Did you mention your concerns about Emily's family to DCI Hillier?"

"He didn't give me the chance to say much at all. I was hoping to talk everything through with him today to look for other similarities."

Steve looked back at his notes and frowned. After what seemed an age, he looked up with his customary smile hovering around his lips, and asked, "Why do you think there is a connection to the abduction we're dealing with?"

Fiona slipped out a photograph of Katie and pushed it across the table. "I think the two girls are related. Both fathered by a German called Carston Boker."

Picking up the photograph for a closer look, Steve replied, "I agree there is an uncanny resemblance. Is the grandmother wealthy?"

Fiona thought about the large house Melanie owned, conveniently near her daughter and the smallholding she had purchased for Tasha. "She's not short of a bob or two."

"I'm talking seriously wealthy. Running into millions and acres of land."

"She is comfortably well off, but I don't think she has millions to play with."

Steve studied the photograph of Katie a second time and handed it back. He rested his chin on the palm of one hand and stared directly at Fiona without saying anything.

Feeling increasingly uncomfortable under the piercing stare and wondering if she had a coffee moustache, Fiona looked down to return the photograph of Katie to her file. Once it was securely put away, she said, "Tell me about your case."

Removing his hand from under his chin, Steve said, "If I was DCI Hillier, I would say that there is no connection between the two abductions."

"But what would you say?" Fiona asked, lifting her chin.

"We are also looking at the uncle and aunt in connection to our abduction, but for very different reasons. Do you know who

Alec Rice is?" When Fiona shook her head, Steve said, "As well as being disgustingly rich and connected to all the right people, he is Amber Rice's grandfather. He is currently under the care of an army of private nurses while his family wait for him to draw his last breath. By all accounts, this is a matter of hours or days away rather than weeks or months. As is the family tradition, the eldest grandchild, Amber, is due to inherit the bulk of his estate under the guardianship of her parents."

"I was told she was an only child. If something happens to her, what happens to the inheritance?" Fiona asked.

"The estate will go to her eldest cousin."

"Which is why you think she has been taken by her uncle and aunt."

"That's what DCI Hillier thinks. Initially, he thought it was a blackmail attempt from outside the family. When no demands were received, he shifted his focus to the uncle. At first, these seemed obvious conclusions, but now, I'm not so sure. I'm certainly open to persuasion."

"Why is that?"

"Despite a thorough investigation and search of their property, there isn't a shred of evidence against the uncle and aunt. I've spoken to them several times and sat in on DCI Hillier grilling them. They are already comfortably off and are quite happy with their lot. I would go so far as to say the idea of handling the grandfather's business interests would terrify them and interfere with their bohemian lifestyle."

"So, what do you think of my suggestion? That the two girls are related biologically."

"It's no more implausible than the theory we have been working on, but there's one thing I can tell you for sure."

"Go on."

"There is no way on earth Amber's father is going to risk the inheritance by admitting his daughter is not carrying the pure Rice genes."

"And Amber's mother?"

"Debatable. She seems resigned to accept whatever her husband says. It's unlikely she would contradict him."

"Could I visit them?"

Steve gave Fiona another of his piercing stares. She felt sorry for his suspects. She wasn't sure how long she would hold out in an interview if she had anything to confess. She straightened in her chair and said, "I will contact the family. It would be easier with your department's blessing."

"Against my better judgement, I'll see if they will agree to meet you, but I'm coming with you."

CHAPTER TWENTY-EIGHT

Steve pulled up at electronic gates set into an eight-foot wall. He leaned forward to speak into the intercom. As the gates silently slid open, Fiona said, "The report said Amber was snatched from her garden. This garden! How on earth did they manage that?"

"Are you referring to the newspaper article?"

Fiona nodded as they travelled along the sweeping drive to the imposing Georgian style house. As the trees lining the drive created a strobing effect, she counted eight windows on each of the three floors and wondered how many of the rooms were in use.

"The family were furious about it. There was supposed to be a complete news blackout on the story. DCI Hillier had a fit when he saw it. He's still searching the station for the leak. I wouldn't want to be in their shoes when he finds them." Parking to the side of the house, Steve said, "Don't forget to leave the talking to me. You're here to observe."

Fiona smiled sweetly in response with her fingers crossed behind her back. She was pleased that it wasn't Peter Hatherall sat beside her. He knew her far too well. He would check her hands were in sight and insist she verbalised her agreement before letting her leave the car.

They were greeted at the door by a housekeeper and ushered through a grand marble hallway the size of Fiona's entire house and into a drawing-room. The furniture huddled in the corner near an open fireplace as if ashamed of their failure to adequately fill the vast space. There wasn't a speck of dust, although the room smelt vaguely musty and had the chill of an unused area. With so many rooms to choose from, that was probably the case. While they waited, Fiona walked along the walls looking at the heavy oil paintings. She was no art critic but, she thought them dull and weighed down by ugly, heavy frames even if they were originals. She took a seat when the housekeeper returned with a trolley of hot drinks.

When Adam swished through the door with his wife Lynda dutifully following a few steps behind, he was immediately on the offensive. "Were you responsible for the leak to the newspapers? Have you come to apologise? I have the sort of friends who could make your position precarious, so it had better be good."

"That's not the reason for our visit, today," Steve said. "DCI Hillier is fully investigating the leak. I understand it may not have been via us."

"I don't know who else it could have been. If there had been an important development, I would expect Hillier to update us personally," Adam said, ushering his wife to take a seat while he remained standing, staring down his thin, aristocratic nose.

"I'm sure he would, Mr Rice," Steve said, far more respectively than seemed necessary given the man's allegations in Fiona's opinion. She couldn't help but wonder how Peter would have handled the situation. Gruffly without an ounce of deference, probably. Glancing across at Lynda Rice, sat with her head bowed, she hoped someone had spoken to them separately rather than rely on the husband's insistence the abduction related to the forthcoming inheritance. That was the first thing she would have done.

"Why don't you take a seat," Steve suggested.

Rather than give up the height advantage, Adam pulled a hardbacked chair from the side of the room and glared down on Steve and Fiona. "Out with it then."

As Adam's glare was focussed on Steve, Fiona watched Lynda Rice, nervously wringing her hands while she perched on the edge of her seat. Her clothes and hair were classy and styled to perfection like her husband, but her face revealed anxiety while his was haughty and aloof. She stared steadfastly on the floor, so there was no chance to catch her eye.

Fiona felt herself blush when she heard Steve introduced her as a colleague from another station, and Adam's cold, calculating eyes bore into hers.

"DI Williams is from Birkbury station. She is dealing with the abduction of a child living in Brierley. It may be connected to your daughter's disappearance."

Adam patronisingly said, "Highly unlikely, one would have thought." Looking across at his wife, he asked, "Do we know anyone from that area?" When his wife shook her head, he stood and said, "We are sorry to hear of another missing child, but I fail to see how it could be relevant to our situation. We are extremely busy people, so I will call for someone to see you both out."

Taking a deep breath to release the pressure to avoid steam emerging from her ears, Fiona pulled out a photograph of Katie and showed it first to Lynda and then Adam. Lynda gasped, her hands shooting to her mouth while Adam demanded to know how she had obtained a photograph of his daughter.

In clipped tones, Lynda said, "That isn't our daughter."

"It's the irrelevant, missing child from Brierley," Fiona said, before placing the photograph face up on the table to the side of her. She pulled out the photograph of Carston Boker. "Do either of you recognise this man?"

Lynda's eyes widened in surprise while her husband stepped forward, snatched up the photographs and shoved them into Fiona's hands. "We don't recognise either of these people and can't help you with your enquiries. That's the correct terminology, isn't it?"

Returning the photographs to the file, Fiona asked, "Was your daughter conceived naturally, Mr Rice?"

Adam's face darkened. Giving Fiona a filthy look, he said, "What an outlandish thing to say. Of course, she was. It is time you left with your utter nonsense." Looking up at Steve, he added, "I will be speaking to your boss. You can expect to find yourself back in uniform by tomorrow."

Turning her back to Adam, Fiona asked Lynda, "Was your daughter conceived naturally? It could help us to …."

"Stop! Stop right there, young lady," Adam demanded. "Get out of my house, now. How dare you upset my wife like this. We've answered your questions. I have no idea what sick game you think you are playing. Our daughter was conceived naturally. Go!"

Fiona squared up to Adam. "I am not playing a game. I am trying to save two little girls who are probably petrified right now. Answering my question honestly will help me to do that." Turning to Lynda, she said, "I'm sure you want the safe return of your daughter as quickly as possible."

Adam grabbed Fiona by the shoulder and swung her around to face him. "What are you implying? We've told you the truth, haven't we, darling? I'm just thankful we have DCI Hillier handling our case, not some slip of a girl who clearly was dragged up without learning any manners. Do I have to call him to get you removed from my house?"

Fiona raised her chin to meet Adam's glare. "Take your hand off me before I arrest you for assault."

With his eyes still blazing, Adam removed his hand and made a point of wiping it clean on a handkerchief.

"We'll see ourselves out," Fiona said. Hoping Lynda was watching her, while Adam was concentrating all his anger on staring her out, she slipped a business card under the base of the table lamp on the nearby table.

Fiona stepped away and raised a hand defensively as Lynda sprang from her chair. She felt the whoosh of air on the side of her face as the sound of the perfectly aimed slap of Adam's face echoed around the room.

"You bastard!" Lynda said, before rushing out.

❖ ❖ ❖

Fiona's flash of temper started to cool as they walk towards

Steve's car. It wasn't the first time she has been thrown out of a house following an interview, but previously the cause had been Peter's bedside manner or rather his lack of it. She hoped Adam didn't see her slip her card under the lamp. The slap told her he was lying to protect the inheritance, but she needed to know more. She was sure they both recognised Carston, and for the startling similarity between the two girls, they had to be related in some way. Even if the card was missed, she thought there was a good chance Lynda would call the station asking for her. If she didn't, she would ring the house and hope she answered rather than Adam.

Steve wrenched open the driver's door and slammed it shut after getting in. He started up the engine as Fiona scrabbled to reach the passenger seat before being left behind. They drove out of the gates in uncomfortable silence.

Fiona pulled out her phone to ring Silton station. "Hi, when we spoke before, you said Dr Jeffrey received an allowance from a trust fund following the death of a relative? Can you check whether that relative was connected to the Rice family in Foxley?"

Once Fiona had put her phone away, Steve glared across at her and said, "What the hell happened to you letting me handle things?"

"I'm sorry," Fiona said, "but all he cares about is the inheritance. You said yourself he was never going to voluntarily admit his daughter wasn't carrying the fine genes of the family. Quite frankly, I think that's a bonus."

"I don't recall him admitting anything. I do remember him telling you repeatedly the opposite and then throwing us out of his home."

"What do you think Lynda's slap was? I think she will be in contact very shortly."

"Or is that just wishful thinking because it fits in with your preconceived ideas? I agree the girls look incredibly alike, but maybe the parents are telling the truth. Everyone is supposed to have a doppelganger. Maybe for some odd reason, you don't want to believe these children were conceived naturally."

Fiona was momentarily stunned. Could that be true? Ever since she had seen the egg next to Emily's body, her unconscious mind had become obsessed with it. Was her mind working the way it was because …? She would never say it out loud, but she had thought recently that she wanted a baby. She considered the thought ridiculous and had purged it from her mind, but the fact remained she had thought it. Even if only fleetingly. Was her biological clock distorting her judgement?

Concentrating her mind back on the conversation, Fiona said, "No. That's absolutely not true. Lynda slapped her husband for a reason. Having her daughter returned is more important to Lynda than the money. It's not as if they are struggling to get by."

"Even if you are correct, do you think she will go against her husband's word?"

"For her daughter, yes."

"When I'm freezing on street patrol, I will warm myself up with that thought."

"Oh, come on," Fiona said. "Surely his threat was all just hot air. He can't have that much control."

"He has DCI Hillier's ear, and that's all he needs to get me kicked off the team."

"If I'm correct, and his wife comes through with the evidence we need to find the girls, you will be the hero who found her."

"I'm not sure Adam Rice will care too much if the inheritance is passed to his niece. And what if DCI Hillier is correct? This is all about the money, and the physical likeness between the two girls is a random coincidence."

"You can't believe that! Not after Lynda's reaction. Anyhow, by all accounts, Adam's father is at death's door. Is he really likely to change his will at such a late stage?"

"Who knows how these families work? But keeping everything in the family is how they hold onto their wealth. I wouldn't put it past him if he is anything like his son."

"If their daughter never returns, the money will pass to the niece anyway," Fiona pointed out before they lapsed into silence for the remainder of the journey.

CHAPTER TWENTY-NINE

After Fiona updated Peter, he told her she might as well head straight home. She thought it likely DCI Hillier would be complaining about her by the time she pulled onto the motorway, so she happily agreed. It gave her the perfect opportunity to have the long-overdue conversation with Stefan. She was still brooding over whether the only reason he had turned up on her doorstep was that he had given the address to the woman who had seen his sister.

She stopped to pick up a couple of bottles of wine. She considered calling Stefan to say she was on her way before deciding she would surprise him. Rounding the final corner, she was relieved to see his car parked a short distance from her home. She grabbed the wine and took a deep breath in front of her front door.

The door opened, surprising them both. Stefan had his overnight bag slung across his shoulders. He dropped it to the floor and stepped back to allow Fiona into the hallway.

Fiona left her keys and the wine on the hallway table before turning to face Stefan. "Going somewhere?"

"I think it is for the best, don't you?"

"You mean you've given up waiting for your sister to contact you here?"

Stefan's shoulders slumped. "If this is what you wish to think, this is up to you."

"It's why you came here and why you're now leaving, isn't it?"

Fiona persisted, unable to resist the blaze of anger.

"I could have given many different addresses."

"But you chose mine without asking. Without thinking whether I minded. You used me like … You are like a sailor with a girl in every port for all I know."

Stefan swooped up his bag. "This is not true. I came here to see you. To have a nice time."

"Oh, gee. I'm so grateful you chose me this time."

"You have serious issues, Fiona. You should sort them out. You will end up a very lonely lady."

"Well, thanks for that." Glancing at the bag, Fiona said, "You weren't even going to bother saying goodbye. Just waltz out like last time, leaving me not knowing where you are."

"This is no longer your concern, and I do not have time for this. Like you do not have time for me. Always work and Peter for you."

Fiona walked back towards the front door and pushed it wide open. "I'm not stopping you from leaving." As Stefan walked by, she added, "And don't come back, again."

Stefan carried on walking without a backward glance as Fiona bit back angry tears. She slammed the door shut and took the wine through to the kitchen. Maybe he was right. She was destined to end up bitter and alone. Looking through the drawer for a bottle opener, she thought if that was her future, she might as well start embracing it.

After gulping down a glass of wine as if it was water, she decided to pull herself together. She put the bottle in the fridge and grabbed a notepad and pen to start jotting down ideas. With the pen poised above the page, she accepted this was who she was. The last girly swot, determined to think her way out of every problem. Her work was more than a distraction. It was the way she survived.

Blanking out the pointless navel gazing, she concentrated on the case and started to jot down her thoughts. Because of the age difference, Katie Clifton and Amber Rice weren't twins, but she was convinced they were at least half-sisters. Carston Boker had been in the country when both girls were taken. Was he collecting the girls he fathered?

She hadn't misread the situation in that draughty drawing room. Lynda Rice recognised the picture of him. She had a sneaking suspicion that so did her pig of a husband. Steve was correct when he said Adam would never admit he wasn't Amber's father. She wasn't so sure about Lynda. She checked her phone, but there were no missed calls.

Fiona tapped her pen on her cheek. The girls' resemblance was so uncanny they could be full sisters. There had been something in The Merrion Clinic's brochure about embryonic transfer.

If Carston was the father, he might know who the mother was. They only had his word that his involvement was limited to handing over a test tube. Could they be working together to recover the girls they considered their own? While their attention had been on Carston, she could have taken the girls anywhere. No one would bat an eyelid at a woman travelling with two similar-looking, little girls. It would automatically be assumed they were her daughters.

Fiona read back through her notes, questioning her conclusions. She acknowledged her fallibility, and in brackets, scribbled down the woman involved could be Susan.

If they were working together, she doubted the mother would have stayed in England after Carston escaped to Germany. But how would she control the girls? There would have been far too many opportunities for them to run away or call for help in a busy airport or ferry port. Unless she drugged them and claimed they were seriously ill. She grabbed her phone. There can't have been that many sick children travelling out of England during the last week.

While checking who to contact about travel arrangements for sick children, she remembered the egg left in Emily's Garden. Was it left there as a sign? A sign to who? To Susan? To Melanie?

The shrill tone of her phone cut across her thoughts. She answered it, hoping it was Lynda Rice confirming she recognised Carston and had used Dr Jeffrey's services. She didn't need any more proof she was on the right lines, but the team might.

She was disappointed when she heard Peter's voice. He laughingly told her DCI Hillier had made a complaint and she should consider herself reprimanded. She had known Peter would back her up but was relieved all the same. She hesitated over sharing her thoughts with him. Realising the time and how tired she was, she decided to leave it until the morning after she had checked a few more things and constructed a logical argument.

CHAPTER THIRTY

Driving into the station car park, Fiona ran through how she was going to explain her reasoning in her mind. She experienced a twang of irritation seeing Peter's and Abbie's cars parked next to each other. What on earth was wrong with her? First Peter's neighbour who she had raised almost to sainthood despite never meeting her, then a sudden if brief desire to have a child and now being bothered by where Abbie parked her car. Her relationship with Peter was close but had always been platonic, so why the sudden testiness? Was this some sort of displacement from the train wreck of her relationship with Stefan, or had she reached the age where she was at the mercy of her hormones acting in mysterious ways?

Peter and Abbie were huddled in deep discussion over a computer monitor in the corner of the office. They turned and beckoned her over.

Fiona joined them shrugging off her jacket, standing behind them rather than pulling up a chair. "What have you found?"

Peter reached out to pull up a chair for Fiona. "This morning, I sent Rachel out to request items from Emily and Katie we could use for DNA testing."

Taking the seat but pushing it back as she sat, Fiona said, "Has Carston agreed to offer up his DNA?"

Peter nodded, before saying, "We've just discovered a DNA check on Katie has been requested before."

"By Tasha Clifton," Abbie said.

"The test confirmed Emily is not her mother. We'll still request our own tests to make doubly sure," Peter added.

Fiona asked, "Anything to suggest who Katie's mother was?" Running her hands through her hair which was still damp from her morning shower, she said, "It's not somebody we know, is it? It's not Tasha? Or Susan?"

"As the sequencing is so different, it's unlikely to be Tasha, but we'll check," Abbie said.

Has anything else come in?" Fiona asked, running the new information through the filter of her late-night research.

"Nothing new. I've been reading some of the material circulated at the extreme edges of pro-life groups," Abbie said. "Only God has the power to give life or sew up a woman's womb."

"What?"

"That's the wording they used."

"But family and friends witnessed Emily's pregnancy," Peter said, still struggling with the idea Emily wasn't Katie's mother. "We discussed this earlier. Susan must have realised."

"Which is where I think Dr Jeffrey comes into the picture," Fiona said. "I did a little more research on her last night. She was at the forefront of championing embryo transfer. We suspected Carston may have been Katie's father because he knew Emily. We now believe if he was, it was via Dr Jeffrey's services. Do you remember the egg left at the scene of Emily's murder? We haven't considered the women involved in the process. The ones who donated their eggs to the programme. What if one of them is reclaiming the children she helped to create? She could even be working with Carston."

"That sounds far-fetched to me," Abbie said. "There are other more straightforward explanations. Even if there is a biological connection, it is via an anonymous fertility treatment. Carston said he never met anyone else and was annoyed because he thought his donation was completely private."

"You do know people sometimes lie," Fiona said, sounding too sarcastic, even to her own ears. So much for her building bridges with Abbie. She could see from the look on Abbie's face the damage was done, so she might as well press on with making her point. "How do you explain Emily and Carston meeting up in a pub? Are you saying that was coincidental?"

"It could have been," Abbie replied. "They were both teachers meeting via another teacher."

"Oh, come on," Fiona said.

Ignoring the jibe, Abbie said, "We don't need to imagine anonymous donors are involved. Some of the extremists refer to embryonic children and say that what fertility clinics do is immoral. I have just discovered the sister checked to see if Emily was Katie's mother. We know she is religious and anti-medical intervention, and there was a history of antagonism between the two sisters."

"Humphries couldn't find anything to suggest Tasha, or her husband have an involvement with the activists."

"That doesn't mean she disagrees with their views. We should be focussing our energy on taking a closer look at the family and Tasha's friend who claims Katie was snatched," Abbie said.

"Tasha killing her sister, then orchestrating the abduction doesn't make sense. She had the child in her home already," Fiona said. "Unless you are suggesting she killed her niece as well because of her beliefs?" Turning to look at Peter, Fiona said, "You said the family liaison officer was good. She thought their shock was genuine."

"Tasha's alibi for Emily's murder has been provided by her family," Abbie said. "They could be lying to protect her."

Fiona stood and paced. "How does Dr Jeffrey and Amber Rice fit into your interpretation? We should be asking what records Dr Jeffrey kept, and why should two girls, with no obvious connection to one another other than their looks, be snatched within weeks of one another?"

Humphries, who had entered the room unnoticed during the argument, said, "It could be there is some weird, satanic, cult thing going on." He shrugged and pulled out a chair when both women glared at him. "Only trying to help."

"Try harder, next time," Peter said. Looking between Abbie and Fiona, he added, "Until the full DNA reports are back, this is all speculation. But if Fiona is correct, it does explain the break-in at the clinic and Dr Jeffrey's murder. She could have been keeping records on certain children, and that was what the person was looking for."

Fiona gave a look to say that she was way ahead, while she continued to pace. "It's the most obvious explanation for why these two children were taken." In a world of her own, she collided with Andrew and Eddie entering the room, carrying a tray of coffees.

"Whoa," Andrew said, raising the tray above Fiona. "Careful." Placing the tray safely on the table, he asked, "What's going on?"

Taking a coffee, Peter asked, "Has anyone checked with The Merrion Clinic whether the Rices were clients?"

Abbie rolled her eyes before wheeling her chair to the next desk. "I will call them and ask."

Fiona said, "You will need to make a formal request in writing to the clinic and it won't achieve anything, if they saw Dr Jeffrey privately. Amber's father will continue to say she was conceived naturally because of the inheritance. I was hoping that Lynda, the mother, might contact me to say something different when her husband wasn't around."

Fiona stopped to answer her phone. Checking who was calling, she raised her fist in a victory salute before wandering to the end of the room. Ending the call, she walked back said, "That was Lynda Rice. She wants to meet me in a café for a chat. I'm fairly confident she will admit off the record that Amber was not conceived naturally. If she thinks it will lead to her daughter being returned, I think she will tell us everything she knows."

Peter said, "Don't jump the gun. It doesn't mean she consulted Dr Jeffrey privately or otherwise."

"True," Fiona said, "And without any records, we don't know for sure why these two girls were targeted." Fiona stopped in her tracks. "Or whether there are other children at risk."

Peter asked Abbie, "Did you specifically ask Carston whether he knew the identity of any of the women involved in the programme?"

"Yes. To put it bluntly, he went in, read a porn magazine,

handed over his sample and waited for his payment to arrive."

"Assuming they did meet up purely because they were teachers, how did Emily know of his *generous donations*?" Peter asked. "It's not the usual type of conversation that crops up between two people who barely know each other."

"I don't know how these things work," Fiona said. "Are you given photographs and a list of attributes so you can pick and mix the genes you want? Emily could have recognised him, from a catalogue."

Peter shrugged. "There's some interesting research for someone." After drumming his fingers on the desk, he said, "Abbie, when Rachel arrives, I want you two to visit Tasha to see what she has to say about her DNA search and check where she was at the time of the clinic's break-in and Dr Jeffrey's murder. Andrew and Eddie, I want you to get hold of Dr Jeffrey's financial records. Check with Silton station how far they went back to avoid duplication. Humphries, how are you progressing with uncovering Susan's real identity? Could she have been the school friend?"

"It's looking more and more likely. All records of India Jennings stop when Susan Penrose took up the university place. She could have reverted to using her real identity when she changed her appearance."

"Fiona. I want you to run with this idea you have. While you are talking to Lynda Rice, I will be requesting full access to the Foxley investigation, and if necessary, suggest we take over the case."

"Good luck with that," Fiona said.

"If needs be, I will make use of our illustrious Superintendent's love of high-profile cases and posing for the cameras." Drumming his fingers on the desk, Peter added, "See if you can link up with the same DI as yesterday. By the sound of it, Hillier gave him a right grilling. As he's already heavily involved in the case, I may slip in a request for his secondment to the team."

"Nothing like rubbing salt into the wound and making things political," Fiona muttered to herself.

CHAPTER THIRTY-ONE

Susan woke with start. She had been dreaming she was at home listening to Emily and Katie giggling in the next room. She jolted and sat upright when she felt the kick. In the dark, her hand instinctively cradled her growing bump ignoring the cold metal of the cuffs on her wrists. She quickly pulled up her T-shirt to feel the solid heel of her unborn baby. Her eyes welled at the momentous occasion of experiencing her baby's kicks. She desperately wanted to share the moment with Emily. Just like she had shared Katie's first kicks when Emily had pressed her hands onto her swollen abdomen.

The chains rattled as Susan pushed the palms of her hands into her eye sockets in a futile attempt to stop her tears from escaping. As they ran down her cheeks, she wiped them away. She couldn't give in to self-pity. She had to stay strong, waiting for the opportunity to escape. For both of them.

Realising the kicking had stopped she swung her legs over the side of the bed and hefted her bulky weight to a standing position. Holding the chains to stop them dragging on the floor, causing the cuffs to dig into her wrists she crossed the carpeted room to the exercise bike. Staring at the windowless, white walls she started to pedal. She focussed on pushing harder on the pedals, letting her mind go blank. Faster and faster. She had to build her muscles and stamina. Sweat started to pour off her as she dropped her head over the handlebars. She ignored her screaming thigh and calf muscles as she pedalled harder and faster.

The single door to the room was flung open with such force it bounced against the wall. Elaine's hand shot out just in time to stop it from smashing into her face. "Get off!" You'll damage my baby."

Susan lowered her head, ignoring the pain in her side and continued to pedal furiously, willing Elaine to move closer. Close enough so she could wrap the chains around her stupid neck and pull them tight with every ounce of her strength.

"You will kill the baby! Is that what you want, you bitch? I already know what a self-centred cow of a mother you would be. There's no need to prove the point to me."

The pain in Susan's side was making it impossible to keep up the pace. It was probably a stitch, but what if it wasn't? What if Elaine was right? She was killing her baby before it had a chance. She slowed her pedalling, keeping her head low, her eyes scanning the floor. She resigned herself to the fact that today wasn't the day that Elaine would take one step too many. She stopped peddling. Not to worry. She was safe until the baby was born. She had six weeks. Or was it five weeks to watch and wait for Elaine's fatal error? She was starting to lose track of time and what if the baby came early? Emily would be doing everything she could to find her, but would it be in time if the baby came early?

"Play the classical music CDs I left for you. I want my baby to have a good start."

Susan heaved herself off the bicycle. She forced herself to walk steadily and not reveal how rubbery and weak her legs felt. She feared they would let her down and send her crashing to the floor at any moment. Would she be quick enough to roll onto her side to avoid damaging her baby? A bout of dizziness caused bile to rise in her throat as she leaned forward to switch on the music, an idea forming in her mind. When she felt stronger, she could fake a fall. That would bring Elaine rushing to her side. And then, one twist and she would have the chains around her neck.

"That's better," Elaine said, closing her eyes and swaying to the music. "Play the foreign language tapes afterwards. Lunch will be served at the usual time."

As the music filled the room Susan's heart sank. What if she overpowered Elaine only to find she wasn't carrying a key to the handcuffs on her? Would she die a drawn-out death without food or water? She shuffled backwards to sit on the edge of the bed. She needed to think through her plans. It wasn't about her anymore. She had to think of the new life growing inside her. It needed nutrients to grow strong and healthy.

From the doorway, Elaine said, "I'll remove the exercise bike if you abuse it again."

Susan lay on the bed looking at the small camera attached to the ceiling as Elaine retreated behind the locked door.

CHAPTER THIRTY-TWO

DI Steve Dowell wasn't pleased to hear from Fiona and sounded dubious when she explained the reason for her call. His attitude had changed when she met him at the pre-arranged spot a short distance from the café.

Steve greeted her with a wide smile and a flash of his perfect white teeth. "Is your DCI some sort of God?"

Fiona could think of numerous ways to describe Peter, but that wasn't one of them. She was more used to defending his brusque manner than accepting praise on his behalf. Even in the station, outside of his team, he wasn't popular. Not that she was, either. It was one of the reasons she felt so comfortable working with him. They were a couple of misfits who had gotten used to each other's moods and ways of working. Instead of replying, she gave Steve a quizzical look.

"I think the purple hue to DCI Hillier's face is going to be permanent. I'm amazed he didn't have a heart attack. You can see the vein near his temple throbbing. I think it's due to the strain of containing so much anger and bitterness. Anyway, enough about him. Let's talk about me. As of now, thanks to your DCI, I'm out of his warpath and temporarily part of your team."

For things to have moved so quickly, Fiona thought it probably had more to do with Superintendent Dewhurst, but she wasn't going to encourage any praise for him. "We tend to call him Peter," is all she replied.

"Peter? Not, Sir?"

Fiona smiled to herself as they walked along. She often forgot the way Peter did things was unusual. "He doesn't use titles and rarely pulls rank. He likes to think of the team as equals working together."

"As soon as we're finished here, I'll be going home to pack. I'm looking forward to it even more, now."

"Is anyone going to miss you? Family, friends, girlfriend?"

"My parents live in Devon. They keep horses, go on long bicycle trips and enter ballroom dancing competitions. I'm not sure they've realised their only son left home years ago."

Fiona wished her parents were so healthy and independent but wondered if Steve's parents worked so hard to fill their days because they did miss him. Typical man, to take everything at face value. She didn't fail to spot he avoided commenting on friends and partners as they continued along the street in companionable silence. She had no intention of asking him anything about his private life.

Opening the door to the café for Fiona, Steve said, "I don't have a significant other. Maybe I'll meet the perfect person in Birkbury."

Half-listening, while thinking he would be disappointed by Birkbury's lack of nightlife, Fiona scanned the tables looking for Lynda Rice. Spotting her sitting in an alcove near the back, she gave a small wave and edged her way through the tables to join her. "Thank you so much for agreeing to see us again."

Lynda half-rose to greet them. "Getting my daughter home safe and sound is all I care about. If that means admitting to some home truths, then so be it. Amber is worth more than all the money in the world." As Fiona and Steve settled in their seats, Lynda continued, "I've decided it's time I put my foot down and stood up for myself. He will never let us leave. Despite everything, I'm not sure I want to. But, once she is home, there are going to be a few changes. I've always envied the nanny my husband employed and the amount of time she spent with her."

"Your daughter was with the nanny when she was taken, wasn't she?" Fiona asked.

"Yes. Amber had been playing in the shade under the oak tree. A tea party of some sort for her dolls. The nanny left her to make them some lemonade. When she returned, Amber was gone."

"How can we contact the nanny?"

"I'm sorry, I don't know. My husband was so angry he fired her on the spot. After a few days, I felt guilty about the way we treated her. When she came to us, she wasn't much more than a child herself, and we had never previously had any complaints. I tried to contact her via the agency, but they said she had gone back home to Romania, and they had no way to contact her."

"Is it possible your nanny had known the abductor? Could she have pre-arranged leaving Amber unsupervised at a set time?" Fiona asked.

"No. I couldn't believe that of her. She loved Amber. She would never do anything to harm her."

Steve leaned forward, "I interviewed her shortly after Amber was taken. She was devastated. She assumed the main gates were locked, so she didn't see the harm in leaving Amber alone while she made them a drink. She was only away for a few minutes."

"Why were the gates unlocked?" Fiona asked.

"My brother-in-law had recently left," Lynda said. "The control panel is in the kitchen. Adam was about to close them when he was distracted by a telephone call. He was ending the call when he heard screams coming from the garden. It's why he is so convinced that his brother took Amber."

"That does make some sense," Fiona conceded. "Does your husband know you are here?"

"No. It's not that he doesn't care about our daughter," Lynda said. "He does in his own way, but he genuinely thinks this is all about money. I sometimes think he has lost his mind. The idea his brother and his wife have taken Amber is ludicrous. Have you met them?"

Fiona shook her head while Steve replied, "A few times."

"Unlike my husband, they are quite happy with their lot. They live like hippies and let their children run riot on their organic farm. They are not interested in the inheritance. My husband can't get it through his thick head that not everyone thinks the way he does. Money doesn't make you happy. In my experience, it seems to do quite the opposite."

Once a waitress appeared and took their order, Lynda confirmed that Amber had not been conceived naturally but via embryonic transfer.

'Yes!' Fiona silently thought. The emotion was one of relief rather than victory. She would leave that until the two girls had been recovered, unharmed. "Do you have any paperwork concerning your pregnancy?"

"I searched through my husband's desk last night after he had gone to bed, but I couldn't find anything." Handing over a slip of paper, Lynda said, "But I jotted down the name and address of the doctor who arranged everything for us. Dr Jeffrey. She was very kind and efficient. And dreadfully discreet. Following your visit, I argued with my husband, suggesting she may have taken Amber. He told me he continued to pay her handsomely for that discretion, so it wouldn't be in her interests, but I still wonder."

"He is correct about Dr Jeffrey. She didn't take Amber," Fiona said, without stating the reason. "How was everything arranged with her?"

Lynda waited to reply while the waitress delivered their three coffees. "My husband handled everything. We could have carried on trying, but he was desperate for us to have the first grandchild. He showed me a photograph of the two donors he had chosen and asked for my agreement."

Fiona pulled out the photograph of Carston. "Could this be the same man your husband showed you?"

After studying the photograph, Lynda said, "Yes. I'm sure of it. That's him."

"And the female donor? What can you tell us about her?"

"She was gorgeous. Petite. I remember she had a mass of bouncy, blonde curls and was smiling a proper smile. One that lit up her whole face. I think Amber will grow up to look very much like her."

"What happened after you agreed to the two donors?"

"I turned up at the allotted time at a house in Berth and was taken up three flights of stairs to a room that looked like any other doctor's appointment room and popped onto a table. The whole thing was over very quickly."

"Did you return for check-ups?"

"No. Once the pregnancy was confirmed, we contacted our own doctor, and things progressed as a normal pregnancy. We never told a soul it wasn't a natural pregnancy. Before you arrived the other day, I had almost forgotten Amber wasn't conceived naturally."

"Would it make such a difference to your father-in-law?" Fiona asked.

"Probably, but the question is academic. He is not expected to last more than a couple of days. My husband fears Amber will lose the inheritance if the truth comes out, because of the will's wording. Although, I wonder if it is as much to do with his pride.

"When you visited Dr Jeffrey, did you see anyone else? A receptionist, maybe?"

"We went late on an evening. Secrecy was all-important, so I assumed my husband had requested there be no one else there. Sorry, I'm not able to tell you more. It isn't much, is it? Will it be enough for you to find her?"

"You've been more helpful than you realise. We will do everything in our power to find Amber," Fiona replied.

Lynda reached across the table and grabbed Fiona's hand. "You do think she's alive? I have this horrible feeling that my husband's first theory is correct, and the blackmail letter hasn't arrived because something has gone terribly wrong."

A tiny sliver of doubt had crept into Fiona's mind when she heard about the brother's visit and the gates being left open. He could have paid the nanny to make herself absent while he grabbed his niece. Amber would have trusted a family member enough to jump into a car without making a fuss. "We will keep an open mind, but I can assure you we are doing everything we can to bring her home to you."

Lynda released Fiona's hand and said, "There is one thing before you go. This other little girl? If she is Amber's biological sister. What happens then? Will they be able to see each other?"

"That will be up to the families to decide, but let's take one step at a time and find them first."

❖ ❖ ❖

At Steve's flat Fiona updated Peter while Steve hastily tidied up mugs and empty beer bottles that were scattered around the living room. After watching him scurry around for a few minutes, Fiona asked if she could make them both a coffee. She found a Bosch coffee machine in the ultra-modern kitchen and set about making the coffee while Steve disappeared into a bedroom to grab some clothes together. Waiting for the coffee machine to do its magic, Fiona wandered back to the living room and took a look around. There was no evidence of a significant other on the scene. There were several photographs of an elderly couple she assumed were his parents either with horses or astride bicycles and some of Steve with a group of male friends huddled around pint glasses in various locations.

Fiona returned to the kitchen and pulled out her telephone to make some calls. She took her first sip of coffee when Steve entered, throwing a heavily laden backpack on the floor.

Steve reached for the coffee mug Fiona had left on the counter for him. "That's me ready. I'll drink this, and we'll be off. I'll follow you. Who are you calling?"

"I wanted to speak to Dr Jeffrey's partner. Unfortunately, Silton station confirmed she has gone to stay with a friend in London. I've called her several times without any luck, so I've left a message asking her to contact me urgently. On our way back, I want to look at the offices Dr Jeffrey used in Berth. It's not far out of our way. You never know she may have left something behind, or someone might remember regular visitors."

They discovered the address Lynda had given them for Dr Jeffrey housed an Estate Agents with a flat above. After ringing the head office, the branch manager confirmed the whole building had previously been registered as a residential property owned by Dr Jeffrey.

They rang the bells on the adjacent houses that were still residential. The few people that answered their door vaguely remembered Dr Jeffrey but had no idea she was carrying out a business from the address.

CHAPTER THIRTY-THREE

After another long, frustrating day, Peter held the daily morning briefing. "Two important developments. The DNA tests have confirmed Carston is Katie's biological father. Her mother is an unknown female. Tasha has claimed she requested the previous DNA out of idle curiosity following a comment made by her mother but has never told anyone the results. Not even her husband."

"And we're accepting that, are we?" Fiona asked.

"Abbie is continuing to look at the family with help from the liaison officer."

"Have we ruled out Susan being Katie's mother?" Eddie asked.

"Why wouldn't she have carried the damn baby?" Fiona said.

"So, it was a shared experience," Abbie replied. "Both would have an equal claim to Katie."

"Today's DNA reports rule out that possibility," Peter said. "We're still waiting for the results from Amber Rice's tests which are being compared to Katie's DNA. We have also located the cottage Susan has been renting. Everything suggests she left the cottage intending to return. We have spoken to the couple who rented the cottage to her and the owners of the local village shop. They have confirmed Susan was heavily pregnant."

Annoyed by the interruption of his phone ringing, Peter rejected the incoming call and slipped his phone into his pocket before continuing. "We know Dr Jeffrey was providing designer babies for couples from an address in Berth. We know Amber

Rice was conceived after using her services and have reason to believe so was Katie. One assumption is that the woman who provided eggs for the programme is recovering what she considers to be her babies and killing anyone who stands in her way. As Dr Jeffrey's records have been taken, we have no idea who she is or whether there are other children at risk." Turning to face the room. Peter said, "Shout out any ideas you have for tracing this woman."

"I've been trying to speak to Dr Jeffrey's partner," Fiona said. "She can't have been totally oblivious to what her partner was doing. She has moved on from London and is currently staying with friends near Chester. I've asked the local station to arrange a house call. They should come back to me later today."

"Okay, any other ideas?"

"Was Dr Jeffrey working alone?" Steve asked.

"We don't know. The set-up costs must have been high," Peter said.

"So were her prices," Eddie said. "We haven't been able to untangle much from her financial records. It looks like most transactions were in cash."

"Okay, we need to look into the possibility she wasn't working entirely alone," Peter said. "Any more ideas?"

"Could we put out a general request for parents connected to Dr Jeffrey at the relevant time to come forward?" Humphries asked.

"That's an option I've already considered and discarded."

Fiona looked up in surprise. "Wouldn't press coverage help us to locate Dr Jeffrey's other patients?"

"During her career, she has worked with hundreds of parents, privately while working at renowned clinics and via the NHS. The sort of request Humphries is suggesting would cause panic. We would be inundated with calls from parents who had nothing to worry about, which would only hinder us locating the small number of children who might be at risk."

"Not necessarily," Fiona said. "The request could be directed at patients who saw Dr Jeffrey at the private address in Berth."

"We have no idea how many parents Dr Jeffrey saw at that

address or how many different donors she used. My point above stands. I see no point in panicking every parent with a blonde, blue-eyed child. Also, the press hasn't picked up on any connection between the two girls, and I would like it kept that way. Any other ideas?"

Fiona shook her head, convinced Peter was wrong but held her tongue.

"How did Dr Jeffrey recruit the donors?" Steve asked.

"The parents are paying for discretion and perfect babies, so there is a premium for attractive looks and high IQ. Carston was a teacher and university students are often used. So, within the educational bubble, although we can't assume there weren't other channels used. Susan Penrose may have played a part in recruitment."

"I see Carston has been ruled out of the investigation, but is he able to identify anyone else involved?" Steve asked.

"No. He went to the top floor of, we think, the same townhouse as Lynda Rice, did the business, and left. Only Dr Jeffrey was present," Abbie said.

"One thing I can't understand," Eddie said, "is why now?"

"Hormones," Humphries suggested.

Fiona gave him a withering look, before saying, "Possibly she has recently discovered she has become infertile?"

"Could we obtain a list of women receiving this news in the last few months?" Steve asked.

"The woman we want to find could be living anywhere in the country, so that would include thousands of women," Peter said. "Even if we could narrow it down, there would be a confidentiality issue. I agree it is likely that something traumatic happened. Otherwise, why wait until the children were already developing personalities and attached to their parents? If she took them as infants, they would grow up knowing nothing different."

"Maybe, she didn't like the idea of sleepless nights and dirty nappies," Humphries said.

"Be serious, can't you?" Peter snapped. "We've two murdered women and two terrified little girls out there somewhere."

"Sorry. Gallows humour," Humphries said.

"Anything could have set up the chain of events, from the death of her parents to a violent assault," Rachel said.

"If the catalyst was her discovering she's now infertile, either due to delaying starting a family or because of the egg donation procedures, that works in our favour," Fiona said. "If she's building a family, she's less likely to harm the girls. That gives us more time to find them."

When his phone rang again, Peter snatched it out of his pocket. "Is it important, Sykes? I'm in a briefing ... Oh, okay ... I'll be right down ... put him in interview room three and offer him a drink." Ending the call, he said, "This could be nothing or the breakthrough we've been waiting for. Can you all wait here? I'll let you know which it is straight away. Fiona? Can you grab photographs of Carston, Katie and Amber, and come with me?"

In the corridor, Fiona asked, "Who is it?"

"Someone I've been trying to get hold of for days. His sister said he was recruited by Susan into the sleep programme when he was at university in Berth."

"Why is that important?"

"He broke up with his long-time girlfriend at around the same time. The sister thinks the split was due to her being recruited by Susan Penrose into an entirely different programme. She didn't know what the programme was, only that her brother was furious. It could have been egg donation or something totally irrelevant. We won't know until we speak to him."

Approaching the interview room, Fiona said, "Even if we discover the ex-girlfriend was involved, without Dr Jeffrey's records, we will still be completely in the dark as to which children are at risk. There must be some way we can use the press to help us."

"I think using them will be a hindrance rather than a help in this case. We know Emily claimed she conceived naturally. So did Lynda initially. Complete privacy may have been a motivator for other couples to seek the services Dr Jeffrey was offering. Those parents, the very ones we want to reach, are the least likely to come forwards."

"Or they might provide the information we need," Fiona said.

"I will give it some more thought, okay," Peter said, before opening the door to the interview room.

A red-haired, green-eyed man, dressed in black jeans and a button-down, paisley shirt, was lounging in one of the chairs. With a window overlooking the high street and chairs not bolted to the floor, the room was used for witnesses rather than suspects. Despite these concessions, it remained a sterile, uninviting space. When they entered, the young man greeted them with a relieved look.

Peter took a seat opposite and introduced Fiona. "Thank you for coming in. Gerry, isn't it? Have you been offered a drink?"

"I'm fine. I'm hoping this won't take long. I'm only here to stop you pestering my sister, so she'll stop pestering me. What is it you want to know? Pippa said it was something about an old friend of mine."

"An old girlfriend."

Pushing his floppy fringe from his eyes, Gerry said, "I've had a lot of them. Which one?"

"Elaine. The girl you dated at school and followed to Berth university."

Gerry's face darkened. "Oh, her. No wonder Pippa didn't tell me what this was about." He stood up to leave. "Sorry, I can't help you. I haven't seen or heard from her in years."

"We're more interested in what happened between the two of you at university," Peter said. "What was her surname?"

Gerry shrugged and wandered over to the window, saying nothing as he looked outside. Turning, he asked, "Am I free to leave?"

"Please," Fiona said, indicating he should return to the table. "Two children are missing. We need your help to find them. Or rather, we need Elaine's. We think she might hold some vital information."

Gerry glanced back at them, and said, "I don't know anything about any children or how on earth you think I could help you find a woman I haven't seen in years."

Fiona caught a frown crossing Gerry's face before he turned away to look out of the window. "Two blonde little girls. They are only six years old." Opening the file, she pulled out the photographs of Katie and Amber and placed them on the table. "Both taken while playing outside. Their parents are frantic. Can you tell us anything that would help find them?"

With his back still to the room, Gerry said, "Elaine White, but she married shortly after we split up to someone called Black. I wasn't lying when I said I haven't seen her for years." Crossing the room, he said, "Can I go, now?" The colour drained from his face, and he shot backwards. "Jesus! Why are you showing them to me?"

Fiona and Peter exchanged a confused look, before Peter asked, "Do you know these two girls?"

Keeping away from the table, Gerry shook his head. "I've never seen them before."

"A bit of an overreaction to seeing their photographs, then," Peter said.

"It took me by surprise, is all. I've never been in any trouble with the police before. I thought maybe you were going to show me pictures of them mutilated or something."

"Mutilated? Why would they be mutilated?" Peter asked.

Fiona touched Peter's arm, before asking, "Did they remind you of someone? They look very similar, don't they?"

"Whatever has happened to them, it has nothing to do with me," Gerry said, still backing away from the table, his face ashen.

"They remind you of Elaine, don't they?" Fiona persisted.

"If you're thinking … the girl I knew would never …."

"Never what?" Fiona asked. "Why don't you sit back down and tell us what you're thinking? We need to get these girls back to their families."

"Can you turn the pictures over?" Once Fiona had done as Gerry asked, he retook his seat looking far less relaxed than earlier. "Yes, okay. They are the spit of Elaine when she was younger. I honestly have had no contact with her since we split, but I find it hard to believe she would ...."

"Would what?"

"It's obvious you think she has taken these children. Why are you speaking to me anyway and not her husband, Simon Black?"

Fiona was momentarily distracted when Peter got up and shot out of the room. Turning her attention back to Gerry, she asked, "Why did you split up? Your sister said you wouldn't talk about it."

"So? I don't discuss my relationship issues with my little sister. Hardly a crime."

"No, but she said you were upset at the time. Something to do with a university research programme?"

Looking defeated, Gerry asked, "What do you want from me?"

"Can we start with why you broke up with Elaine and move on from there?"

"She changed once we moved up to university. One thing I always loved about her was the way she cared for her younger brother, Alec. He had Down Syndrome, but she treated him like everyone else. She hung out with him at school and invited him up to stay weekends during her first term. That year, she went from being a caring, top sister to denying he even existed."

Peter had the girl's full name and was no doubt ensuring everyone was looking for her. Until he returned, Fiona decided to let Gerry carry on at his own pace, to see where it went.

"A group of us were chatting about what to do for her upcoming birthday. When I mentioned Alec coming, she dug her fingernails into my hand under the table and turned her head so no one else could hear her say, 'I don't have a brother.' There were other things. She became snobby and moody. I thought she had gotten herself involved in drugs. The thing with her brother was the final straw."

The door to the interview opened, and Peter retook his seat while Gerry continued talking. "We argued that night about her changed attitude and how she had suddenly become ashamed of her brother. That's when she told me what she was doing and where all the money was coming from."

"Which was?" Fiona asked.

"Repeatedly donating her eggs. It involved her taking drugs to keep them coming. She said that was why she was moody, but she needed the money. She was worried that if they knew about her brother, they might drop her from the programme."

"That was when you split up?" Fiona asked.

"Pretty much, yeah. We may have gotten back together, but shortly after we argued that night, she dropped out of uni. I've no idea where she went except not home. I tried numerous times to speak to her. She didn't return any of my calls, so in the end, I gave up trying. I honestly have never clapped eyes on her since."

"But you knew she married shortly later," Peter pointed out.

"She sent wedding invites to a couple of friends. I think they went. I wasn't invited. I wouldn't have gone if I had been."

"Do you know who ran the programme and how she became involved?" Peter asked.

"I assume it was Susan Penrose. I don't remember her mentioning any other names."

"Do you have any pictures of Elaine?" Fiona asked.

"Good grief! No. I'm not in the habit of keeping pictures of my exes. I expect she's changed, anyway. I doubt I would recognise her if she walked past me in the street tomorrow."

❖ ❖ ❖

When they concluded the interview and escorted Gerry out of the station, Humphries followed them at a discrete distance. As the door swung shut behind Gerry, Humphries said, "Simon Black reported his wife missing four months ago. Also, Superintendent Dewhurst is looking for you."

"Great. Does he know I'm in the building?" Peter asked.

"Yes."

"While I go and see why he's looking for me, I want you two to go straight out to interview Simon Black."

CHAPTER THIRTY-FOUR

Susan didn't know what had woken her. She put it down to a stomach cramp or a strong kick. Her baby was most active in the early evening. Thinking about it, she hadn't felt her moving about most of yesterday. She reached down to cradle her bump. Reassured everything was how it should be, she stretched out on her back and stared at the ceiling. Rubbing her hand over her swollen stomach, she turned away from the camera and whispered, "Somehow, I'm going to get us out of here. I can't wait for you to meet Emily and your big sister, Katie. They are going to adore you."

For the hundredth time, she ran through the events that had led to her being chained to a bed. With all the time in the world, she didn't start the narrative on the day she approached Dr Jeffrey. She traced it all the way back to the event that shaped her adult life.

She laid all the blame at the foot of her cowardly, spineless father. Like all men, when it came to the test, he thought only of himself. Now she was about to be a mother, his actions seemed even more unfathomable. He worshipped her mother, but so did she. She was equally devastated when cancer took hold of her mother and killed her within six short months. To take his own life when his only daughter needed him was unforgivable. The fact he hadn't asked anyone to care for her and had hung himself when she was sleeping in the next room was the icing on the cake. The horror of discovering him still gave her nightmares.

As her parents were both only children, she was totally alone trying to process everything. A few weeks shy of her eighteenth birthday, she had slipped through the system. She had gone from a happy, well-adjusted girl with two loving parents to having no one. She turned up to take her A levels and set off to university, just as she had planned. Except she used the name of her friend who had been killed in a car accident that summer. Her friend's grades were better than hers, and with her new name, she could start a brand-new life. And since meeting Emily, it had been a wonderful life, until now.

Emily was the only person she had ever told about her parents and taking on a new identity. She was the only person who fully understood why she couldn't allow Katie to be an only child. To provide her with a biological sister was everything. Dr Jeffrey had been reluctant, but never in her wildest dreams did she think Elaine would come looking for her and claim a right to her unborn child.

Adjusting her position, she felt the cold wetness of her nightdress. Her eyes widened, and fear gripped her as she checked under the duvet. Her heart started to beat rapidly as she felt a moment of light-headiness. Her waters had broken. It was too soon. She had another four or five weeks, didn't she? She wasn't ready.

She should be at home with Emily beside her, ready to grab the pre-packed suitcase and rush her to the hospital where she would be taken care of. She had written her birth plan. It shouldn't be happening this way. It couldn't.

Taking deep breaths to calm herself, she knew she had to do something. Like it or not, and she most definitely did not, the only person who could save her baby was Elaine. She turned to face the camera and started to shout, "Help! My waters have broken."

She seemed to have been shouting for hours when Elaine finally opened the door. She stayed by the door, and called out, "Show me."

Susan wasn't sure she should move. Would standing upright

make the situation worse as gravity took over? She had no choice as Elaine wasn't moving from the doorway. Had she somehow read her mind all the times she planned to fake a fall so she could grab her when she ran over to assist? Or worse. Had being locked in the room alone driven her crazy? Had she been voicing her thoughts out loud without realising? Slowly she sat up, pulled back the duvet and swung her legs over the side of the bed. Perching on the end, she held up her sodden nightdress.

"Are you experiencing any contractions?" Elaine said as calmly as a trained midwife.

"I don't think so."

"No sudden stomach cramps or pains?"

"I'm not sure. Something woke me up, but I don't remember feeling anything at all." Looking down at herself, she said, "It just appeared."

"Lie back down. I will have to examine you."

Susan carefully manoeuvred herself into position. She held her breath and screwed her eyes tightly shut to block out the indignity of an examination. Instead of approaching footsteps and rough hands touching her and making her skin crawl, she heard the click of the door close and the turning of the lock. She pulled the duvet over herself, hoping and praying Elaine had finally come to her senses and was calling for professional help.

Ten minutes later, Elaine returned with a clean nightgown and what looked like a glass of orangeade. She placed them on the floor by the door and said, "I will examine you once you have drunk this."

Susan didn't bother to ask what drugs were in the drink. "Do you know what you're doing?"

Elaine nodded. "I won't let anything happen to my baby. It's early, but if it has to be delivered now, so be it."

"Of course, it needs to be delivered. My waters have broken."

"Not necessarily. I can give you something to slow things down. There are antibiotics in the drink. Drink it," Elaine ordered, before retreating behind the door.

Susan eased herself off the bed. She knew Elaine would be

watching via the camera. Was this the time to feign drinking and pretend to fall unconscious? Or would that endanger her baby?

CHAPTER THIRTY-FIVE

Fiona's phone rang as they pulled up outside Simon Black's home. "That was Peter. The lab confirmed Katie and Amber are full sisters."

"A hell of a way to discover you have a sibling," Humphries replied.

Simon met them at the door, looking dishevelled and anxious. His clothes looked and smelled like he had slept in them, and the dark stubble on his face matched the dark rings under his eyes. "Have you found her? You said on the phone new information had come to light."

"Can we come in?" Fiona asked.

They were led through a wide, airy corridor to a sunroom overlooking the garden. The sliding doors were open, the design allowing the indoors to merge with the outdoors. Decking gave way to a large lawn leading to a small orchard. The borders were lined with a mature hedge and an abundance of flowering plants. Taking her seat, Fiona said, "You've a lovely garden."

Hovering by the glass doors, Simon said, "Thank you. It's why we bought the house."

Looking down the garden, Fiona caught sight of a treehouse built into the trees with a rope ladder hanging beneath. It was something she always longed for growing up. A secret place high up in the trees away from grownup's prying eyes. "Who built the treehouse?"

"I built it. We had hoped to fill the house with children. Unfortunately, that hasn't happened. Can I get you something to drink before we start? I'm sure you're not here to talk about garden design."

"We're fine," Fiona replied, accepting no amount of small talk was going to relax him. "We would like to talk about your wife's disappearance. We understand she was suffering from depression before she left."

"Yes, I've already discussed this with the other officers. They concluded as she was an adult and left of her own accord, there was nothing more they could do."

"What caused the depression?"

"How many more times do I have to go through this?" Simon asked, looking annoyed. After an exaggerated sigh, he continued, "She was very down after her brother died. She blamed herself, which was ridiculous. But that's the way she is. Always caring for others and taking on too much."

"I know you've been through all this before, but could you take us through what happened to her brother? Having a clear idea of her state of mind will help us to find her."

After a short pause, Simon continued, "Elaine always encouraged her brother to become more independent despite his disabilities. We helped him move out of the family home and into an assisted living arrangement. The project was fantastic. As well as housing, the group organised a part-time job for him. The last time we met him, he was bubbling over with excitement and pride. No one could have predicted what was going to happen. Least of all, Elaine, but she didn't see it that way."

"What happened?" Fiona asked.

"Covid spread through the shared house. Several of them were hospitalised, but he was the only one to die."

"I see. I'm sorry for your loss."

"At the same time, we were trying for a family. I think Elaine thought she would fall pregnant as soon as we started trying. Before her brother's death, she stayed upbeat about things not happening straight away. Afterwards, her mood fell a little lower with every monthly cycle."

"How long had you been trying for a family?"

"The last few years. We both wanted to be secure in our careers first. I told her to relax, and it would happen, but she became more and more anxious as the months progressed. She visited her doctor the morning of her disappearance. She hasn't been seen since."

"Do you know what was discussed with the doctor?"

"He won't release full details of his examination without a court order, but he explained to Elaine why she wasn't conceiving. The police didn't think the case warranted applying for the order once they discovered she had cleared out our savings account. When the branch confirmed she had gone in personally, they stopped suspecting me of her murder. It's not a good feeling, you know. Being suspected of killing the most important person in your life."

Fiona felt sympathetic, but she knew it was standard practice and sadly, it often turned out that the partner was responsible. Her thoughts wandered to the two small girls. She hardened her resolve and asked, "How much was in the account?"

"Nearly fifty thousand."

Fiona took a sharp intake of breath. That much money gave Elaine far too many options to stay hidden. "Did Elaine talk about her time at Berth University? You must have met her shortly after she left."

"Not really. The experience left her with lasting scars."

"Oh?"

"She was bullied by housemates and an ex-boyfriend. They virtually hounded her off the campus. That's why she dropped out. She's always regretted not standing up to them at the time. Although she enjoyed her work as a teacher assistant, she felt she could have done more with her life, if it wasn't for them." Simon abruptly stood and said, "I've been over all this before. Do you have new evidence? Why are you so desperate to find her now?"

Avoiding the question, Fiona said, "We will be speaking to the school and the teachers she worked with. Was there anyone, in particular, she was friendly with or disliked maybe?"

Simon shrugged. "She was … is a private, reserved person. We both are. She thought she would have made a far better teacher than most of the ones she worked with. So, no, she didn't socialise with them. She cared more for her students. She loved children and wanted a big family. That's why the problems we experienced hit her so hard. I told her, over and over again, not to worry. I would be happy to undergo fertility treatment if that was what was needed. My appointment to be assessed was booked for the day after she disappeared, so I didn't go. I told her we could adopt or foster. None of it is an issue for me. I just want her home and happy."

"Did she have a favourite place to go? Somewhere you went on holiday, maybe? A place of happy memories?"

"You think I if I knew of a place like that, I wouldn't have gone there already to look for her?" Collapsing back onto his chair, Simon said, "No, nothing springs to mind. We usually go somewhere different abroad every year."

"Did your wife take her passport with her?"

Simon shook his head. "No, it's here. I can show it to you if you like."

"That's okay. How about family holidays when she was a child?"

"Her parents had a caravan near Bournemouth somewhere, but that's long gone. You would have to ask them exactly where it was. Her mother was a keen walker, and they sometimes drove out on weekends for long walks. She has also given all this information to your officers. You haven't answered my earlier question. Why are you so keen to find her now? I thought you had given up."

"We believe she may have been involved in another crime."

"She's not hurt, is she?" After reading Fiona's expression, Simon said, "Elaine? You must be kidding. She doesn't even have a speeding ticket. What sort of crime?"

"I can't disclose that information," Fiona said. "Did she leave her toothbrush or a hairbrush behind when she left?"

"Both." A light bulb came on behind Simon's eyes. "I watch television. I know why you want them. I won't hand them over until you tell me what she has supposed to have done."

174

"We could obtain a court order, but that would only delay things. We want to find her before she does something stupid. I assume you want the same."

Simon's eyes darted manically around the room until he dropped his head into his hands. "Okay, I'll go and get them."

"Do you mind if I come with you?" Fiona said, already standing.

Climbing the stairs, Simon mumbled to himself, "Oh God. What have you done, Elaine?" Rubbing his eyes on the landing, he said, "If she has done something bad, then she is ill. When you find her, she will get the treatment she deserves, won't she? She won't be treated like a criminal?"

"She'll receive any medical help she needs," Fiona said diplomatically. After listening to Simon, she felt some sympathy for Elaine, but it didn't excuse murder and abduction. Her priority was finding the girls and ensuring no one else was hurt.

As Simon led her through a double bedroom to the en-suite bathroom, Fiona slipped on her gloves and had an evidence bag ready. "If you could point to her things, I'll take it from there."

Returning downstairs, Fiona asked, "When you talked about fertility treatment, did Elaine ever mention the name of a clinic or a doctor's name? An expert she knew who might be able to help?"

"We hadn't gotten so far as thinking about clinics. Our GP's name is Dr Mansfield. She never mentioned any other doctor."

"Has she ever spoken about an old friend, Susan Penrose?"

Simon shook his head at the mention of the name.

"Did Elaine have a laptop?"

"Yes, the police returned it weeks ago." Nodding in the vague direction of the living room, Simon added, "It's in the cabinet in there. I haven't touched it since it was returned. Do you want it?"

"Please."

Handing the laptop to Humphries, Fiona handed over her card. "If you hear from Elaine or think of anything else that might help us to find her, please contact me."

"Where are you going now?"

"To the school where your wife worked. Someone there might

know something that could help us."
"Will you keep me updated? Please?"
"Of course, we will."

CHAPTER THIRTY-SIX

Jake's cigarette butt joined the others on the ground. He felt sick from chain-smoking so many. He sat on the narrow bench at the bus stop with his head in his hands to wait for his mates. He had promised Elaine not to tell anyone, but that was before the police arrived. He needed to speak to someone who could tell him what to do.

"Hey, Jake. You are so dead," Trent said.

"What were you thinking, running out of class like that? They're making a big deal about you missing afternoon class and going crazy trying to find you," Ben said.

"And they rang your mum," Trent announced, sitting down beside him. "Hey, budge up."

Jake pulled out a battered packet from his blazer pocket and lit another cigarette. That's all he needed. More grief from his mother.

Leaning against the Perspex walls, Trent asked, "So what gives?"

Jake leaned his head back and blew out a smoke ring. Poking the middle of it with his finger, he said. "I know stuff."

"Yeah, like what stuff?" Ben asked, lighting a cigarette.

"Definitely not the garbage we just sat through. Double history." Pretending to stick his fingers down his throat, Trent added, "With Miss Harper."

"Are you going to tell us what this stuff is?" Ben asked.

"Those coppers who were here today. I should have told them," Jake said through a cloud of smoke.

"Told them what?" Trent asked.

Jake closed his eyes, blowing another smoke ring.

"She was quite tasty. I do agree with you there. I wouldn't mind being banged up in some cell with her for hours," Ben said.

"Idiot." Trent cuffed him around the back of his head. "You would have ended up with giant man, and I bet you would have cried like a baby. Probably wet your pants and all. Given up all your secrets under a little pressure."

"Shut up, guys! I need to think," Jake said. "It's about Mrs Black. That's who they were here about."

"What about her. I know you were the teacher's pet and all. But what gives?" Trent asked.

"I did her a favour."

"Oh yeah," Ben said, gyrating his hips to raucous laughter. "Are you sure she wasn't the one giving you the favour?"

Jake shook his head. "I sorted out a fake ID for her."

"What! She couldn't get served down her local? She don't look that young," Ben said.

"Don't be such a dick. I don't know why she wanted it, and I didn't ask. I overheard one of the other teachers say she has gotten herself in a shed load of trouble. I don't want to be responsible for something bad happening to her. I think I should have said something. You know, to that copper."

"Well, you've missed your chance. They've gone and here's our bus. You should be more worried about skipping double history. Your mum is going to go crazy again when the school contacts her. I bet she calls my dad and says it's all my fault," Trent said.

Climbing the steps into the bus and flashing their passes to the driver, Jake said, "I'll try to stop her, okay. Say I had a migraine or something."

CHAPTER THIRTY-SEVEN

Chrissy Bond held her daughter's hand as they walked to school, trying to hurry her along. Chrissy concentrated on giving the impression she had all the time in the world to listen to Skye's chatter while inside, her stomach twisted into knots. The report, which she should have finished before leaving work to collect Skye from the after-school club yesterday, needed to be completed before her ten o'clock meeting.

They were held up crossing the road by a convoy of cars, most of which would shortly be queuing up, ignoring the hazard warning signs, to park outside the school gates. More infuriating, most of the cars were driven by stay-at-home mothers who had all the time in the world to fritter away. She would speak to her husband again about her giving up work. It would only be for a few years. They might be able to hang onto the house if they economized elsewhere. If they couldn't, she would be happy living in a smaller house if it meant she could spend more time with Skye.

Chrissy huffed, waiting to cross, trying not to think about the build-up of diesel fumes they would be forced to breathe when they rounded the final corner before the school.

"Mummy, you're hurting my hand."

Chrissy released her tight hold. "Sorry, darling, I didn't realise. Quick, now. There's a gap."

Stepping into the road, Chrissy heard the roar of an engine and saw a flash of movement in her peripheral vision. Annoyed that the speed limit around the school was being ignored, she moved to shield Skye and raised her arm to slow the approaching vehicle. As Chrissy turned, a gloved hand shot out, hitting her in the chest. She felt herself falling backwards in slow motion. There was a loud crack when the back of her head hit the pavement, followed by a vacuum of perfect silence. A moment of peace, lying on the ground, her mind emptying. The roar of the engine farther along down the road brought her to her senses. She scrambled to her feet and let out a piercing scream. She was surrounded by a sea of concerned faces, but Skye was gone.

CHAPTER THIRTY-EIGHT

Peter was in a foul mood. Superintendent Dewhurst had caught up with him first thing and offloaded yet another exciting project, as he called them, onto him. After a cursory look, Peter called it a collection of out-of-touch ad re-hashed ideas. He now had wall-to-wall meetings with well-meaning, if misguided, enthusiasts of the scheme to look forward to. The newspaper report that Dewhurst had slammed down on his desk and the slating that followed had been the icing on the cake.

He started the morning briefing by banging a copy of the same newspaper on the front desk. "The press has made the connection between the two abductions. Their report is mostly supposition based on the similarities between the two girls." After a pause, he added, "They somehow know we have questioned a young German teacher who might be their father. Would anybody like to explain how they came by that little snippet of information?"

Fiona shifted in her seat, ignoring the look Peter was giving her. Yes, she was the one who wanted press involvement, but she wasn't the leak. If Peter thought about it, he would know she would never go behind his back like that. She risked a sideward glance at Abbie. Abbie had a history of accidentally leaking details. It was her who flew out to speak to Carston. She was a far more likely candidate. Maybe it was an act of revenge, knowing suspicion would fall on her.

"I explained my reasons for not involving the press. There's a reason for the rules about involving the press and procedures for deciding what to share. It would be easier if whoever it was owns up now." The room remained silent. "Or by the end of the day." Turning to the whiteboard, Peter said, "Let's summarize where we are."

Peter's sum-up served only to highlight Fiona's sense of failure. Any satisfaction from being proved right was overtaken by the frustration of knowing who they were looking for but having no idea where to find her.

She half-listened to the report Abbie was giving. "Elaine had no close friends, and she kept much of her life private from her husband. Peter tracked down several of Elaine's university friends when trying to locate her." Catching Fiona's eye, she said, "I've re-spoken to them, but none could recall any incidents of bullying."

Fiona refused to rise to the bait and comment. This wasn't the time for point-scoring. She hadn't been convinced by the bullying claims in the first place. She had merely passed on what Elaine had told her husband and asked Abbie to check it out.

The room was pulsating with tension and irritation as Peter barked out instructions. Fiona blushed when Peter bluntly told her and Humphries to go back to the school to speak with Elaine's students as they should have done on their first visit. He was about to close the briefing when his telephone rang.

Ending the call, he passed on the news that Fiona had been dreading. "Another similar looking child has been abducted. This time in broad daylight in front of her distraught mother and several other parents dropping their children off for school."

"Do we have a description?" Fiona asked.

"Unfortunately, not. She was wearing a motorcycle helmet. She grabbed the child from her motorcycle and sped off before anyone had time to react."

"Registration number?" Humphries asked.

"All we have is it was a powerful bike and silver in colour. Abbie and Steve get over to Brockeridge village school, now, while the parents are still there. Take Andrew and Eddie with you."

Fiona watched them sail out of the room with a sinking heart.

"You two. Get back to Highcroft School and speak to Elaine's students."

CHAPTER THIRTY-NINE

Heading out to Highcroft School, Humphries speculated about why Elaine had changed from snatching the girls, unseen to grabbing a child surrounded by witnesses. "Could the newspaper report have been the catalyst?"

"Not necessarily," Fiona said. "It could be she has been watching and waiting for a suitable opportunity, but the child has been too closely supervised. Or she was the final child to be recovered, and she was growing impatient to start their new life together."

"Do you think that is her intention?"

"I want to believe it is as it means the girls won't have been harmed. Not physically, anyway."

"She must be bonkers if she thinks they are going to forget all about their families and accept her as their new mother."

"That's the part that concerns me," Fiona said. "We don't know how she is going to react when the girls don't fall into line. They are old enough to object and cry for their parents but not old enough to realise their best bet might be to go along with the crazy until she lets down her guard."

"Who do you think leaked the information to the press? Do you think it was the DI seconded from the Amber Rice case?"

Fiona had been so fixated on considering Abbie as the leak she hadn't thought about that possibility. She liked Steve. He was enthusiastic about joining their team and wouldn't be wanting to upset anyone, but she didn't know him well enough to say he was innocent. "It's unfair to blame the new kid on the block, without any evidence."

"Looks a bit suspicious, is all I'm saying."

"Steve said there was an earlier leak at Foxley station. It could be the same person or someone feeling disgruntled by the way we've taken over the case." Fiona glanced across at Humphries, wondering if he was peeved about returning to the secondary school rather than the scene of the new abduction. "Sorry, you're having to return to the school with me. It was my mistake. I should have insisted on speaking to the pupils yesterday."

"By the time the teachers had all told us what a quiet, caring woman Elaine was it was the end of the school day. If Peter hadn't been in such a cranky mood over the newspaper article, I would have pointed that out."

"Thanks for that, but we should have spoken to some of them," Fiona said. "Do you remember hearing the motorcycle the first time we visited Tasha?"

"I had forgotten about that," Humphries said. "A motorcycle passed the junction when we were waiting to pull out. You don't think …?"

"It's an infuriating thought, but yes."

"And Melanie's neighbour heard a motorcycle starting up," Humphries said, as the realisation of how close they had been to Elaine set in.

"Call Abbie to make sure they ask the parents about recent sightings of a motorcyclist hanging around the area."

"Why don't you speak to her? It might clear some of the friction between the two of you."

"It's that obvious, is it?"

"Umm, yeah," Humphries replied. "I'll call the number for you, shall I? Good for teamwork and all that."

"Go on, then. I'll speak to her."

❖ ❖ ❖

When they arrived at the school, a receptionist commandeered a student to take them to the headmistress' office. After pushing through the first set of double doors, Fiona asked the student, "Do you know Mrs Black?"

Without slowing her pace, the girl replied dismissively, "I know of her. She deals with the dumb ... more challenged kids." The implication from her tone being she was most definitely not in that category. She turned to the right and led them up a flight of stairs. At the top, they started along a long, narrow corridor. The shrill school bell pierced the quiet. Doors were thrown open, and teenagers spilt out from either side, shouting, laughing and pushing as they made their way to their next lesson. Fiona and Humphries stood to one side, allowing them to pass by.

At the sound of a second bell, the corridor emptied as quickly as it had filled, doors slammed shut, and an eerie silence established itself. Their student escort turned and beckoned them on. Stopping by a door, she said, "The head's office is straight on down there. Can I leave you to make your own way? I need to get to class."

"Of course," Fiona replied. She turned to watch her hurry along the corridor. Once she disappeared through the double doors leading to the staircase, a door halfway along the hallway opened. Two boys poked their heads out, looking either way, to check the coast was clear. Their eyes widened in dismay, and their shoulders slumped when they saw Fiona heading towards them, closely followed by Humphries.

"Hi. Planning on taking the rest of morning off?" Fiona asked.

"No ... umm ... Just running a few minutes late," the smaller of the boys replied, looking at his feet, while the taller boy replied, "As if," looking defiant.

"Do either of you know Mrs Elaine Black?"

The taller boy laughed. Pushing the smaller boy forward, he said, "Jake here likes to think he's her favourite student. He has stacks of super-secret info on her."

Turning crimson, Jake pushed his friend's shoulder. "Shut up, already."

Leaning against the wall, the taller boy asked, "So, lady, if we give you the lowdown can you get us out of classes for the day?"

"If you would be happy to answer some questions, I will say it's my fault you missed this class," Fiona said. "Will that do?"

The boys stared at each other without replying.

"What's the class?" Humphries asked.

"Double Geography," the two boys replied, before pulling disgusted faces and groaning.

"Can't say as knowing the difference between a stalagmite and stalactite or knowing how a bow lake is formed ever helped me much," Humphries said.

"How about it?" Fiona asked. "A quiet chat or we find your classroom?"

"Could we take this down the station?" the taller boy said, in an awful attempt at a cockney accent.

"I don't think that will be necessary," Fiona replied. "If that's a yes, give us your names, and we'll clear it with the head."

While Humphries walked off to speak to the head's secretary, Fiona asked, "Could we talk in there?" indicating the door the boys had emerged from.

Jake squirmed before opening the door to reveal a stationery cupboard.

"I guess not," Fiona said, suppressing a smile. "Is there a canteen or somewhere else quiet we could go?"

Dressed in their whites, the kitchen staff glanced up from their table where they were sharing a drink and gossip. All chatter stopped as they eyed the new arrivals with suspicion and annoyance. "You're not allowed in here until after eleven."

Humphries held out his warrant card and flashed his biggest smile, before saying, "We're here on official business." For added benefit, he lied, "The head gave us permission. Could we have a couple of coffees?" Turning to the boys, he asked, "And?"

"A pint would be good, but I guess we'll make do with a couple of cartons of chocolate milk," Trent said.

The woman who had earlier elected herself the spokesperson slowly pushed her chair back to stand. Plonking a white cap on her greying hair, she gruffly said, "Go and sit down somewhere and I'll bring it over."

"Thank you," Fiona said, before leading the group to a table in the far corner. Humphries took up the rear, hustling the boys along who were busy smirking and sticking their fingers up at the annoyed staff.

Settled around the table, Fiona asked, "What is this information?"

"Go on. Tell the nice lady what you told the rest of us," Trent urged.

Jake blushed an even deeper red. "Is she okay? I don't want to create any trouble for her."

"We need to find her as a part of our investigation," Fiona said.

"Her being in danger probably explains it," Trent said, proceeding to pour salt over the table.

Humphries took the salt container from him and asked, "Explains what?"

Jake looked down as the coffees and chocolate milk arrived. After poking the plastic straw in the carton, he said, "She's alright, is Mrs Black. She's helped me loads with words and stuff. I wanted to help her. I won't get in any trouble, will I? If my Mum receives any more grief about me, I will be grounded for life."

"How did you help her?" Fiona asked.

"I made her a false id. I thought maybe she needed to get hold of something a teacher shouldn't."

Trent guffawed. "Like what? Like porn or something?"

"I don't know," Jake said defensively.

Fiona gave Trent a sharp stare before asking Jake, "Do you remember the name on the ID?"

"Yeah. I didn't realise she needed it to disappear. You'll keep her safe from whoever is after her, won't you."

"Probably the husband," Trent said. "It normally is."

Ignoring Trent's assumption, Fiona asked, "What was the name on the ID?"

"Mrs Ellie Gibson."

Humphries startled the boys by standing abruptly. He left the canteen and went out into the corridor, pulling his phone out as he went.

"That's very helpful," Fiona reassured the boys who had turned in their chairs to stare after Humphries. "Did she mention where she might be heading?"

"No," Jake said, still nervously staring after Humphries. "She didn't say she was going anywhere or why she wanted the ID, and I didn't ask. Well, you don't, do you? Question teachers."

Humphries re-joined them at the table and asked, "Did she ask you about false number plates?"

"I just do IDs," Jake replied.

"Do you know anyone who does know about false plates?" Humphries asked.

"Sorry, no."

Sensing hesitation, Fiona asked, "Are you sure? We really do need to find her as quickly as possible."

"There's a guy in Easton," Trent said. "An ex-pupil from here called Nobby. He tinkers about with bikes and cars behind his house. That's the only person I can think of."

"You won't say we said anything, will you?" Jake asked nervously.

"No, this is all off the record," Humphries said. "We'll keep your names out of it."

"Did Mrs Black ever talk about friends or places she liked to go?" Fiona asked.

"No, nothing like that. She's a teacher. We didn't talk about other stuff."

"But she asked you to create a fake ID for her. How did she know to come to you?"

"Months ago, she saw us getting served in a pub and wanted to know how we managed it. She contacted me at home shortly after."

"Which pub, and was she with anyone?" Fiona asked.

"The Queen's Head in Lockington. She was with a bloke. I assumed it was her husband."

The boys gave a description that matched Elaine's husband. They weren't able to give any more information, so they were escorted to their classroom. Heading back out, Humphries said,

"Peter has arranged for a trace on Ellie Gibson. He will let us know as soon as they find anything. The others are still at Brockeridge school, interviewing everyone who witnessed this morning's abduction. The bike was a Royal Enfield Interceptor."

"With false plates, I take it."

"In one."

"We'll head out to Easton to see if we can find this Nobby character," Fiona said.

"Peter wants us to visit the child's mother before we do anything else. She was taken from the scene to Accident and Emergency, but she's back home with her husband now."

CHAPTER FORTY

The Bond's home was an imposing Victorian building in the centre of the high street in the small town of Tarkington. Entrance from the street was via a stone archway where a horse and carriage would have passed through in days gone by. The front door was opened by Rachel, looking harassed. "Come in and join the throng. Family and friends have rushed around, and there's hardly room to move. It's like a party back there."

"Have you managed to talk to the parents alone?"

"No, by the time I arrived at the hospital, both sets of parents and a friend were already there. People have been flooding in ever since we got back."

"Introduce us to the parents, and we'll take them into another room."

"The garden would be your best bet," Rachel replied, leading them into a large, well-equipped kitchen crammed full of people.

The chatter stopped as a sea of inquisitive faces looked towards them. Ignoring the curious looks, Fiona concentrated on finding the parents, Ian and Chrissy Bond. Rachel pointed them out to her. The couple held hands, looking dazed and confused at the far side of the room. They were next to an open door that led out to a small, stone courtyard, where the smokers had congregated.

The Bonds were older than Fiona expected. She guessed them to be in their late forties. After Rachel introduced them, Chrissy Bond immediately asked, "Have you found her?"

"Could we talk somewhere quieter?" Fiona asked. "The rear garden, maybe?"

The couple wordlessly stood and led them out of the kitchen

through a warren of rooms. Fiona thought the décor matched the pallid faces of the occupants, and she wondered how a lively child would fit into the dull space. The colour scheme ranged from white to beige. There wasn't so much as a cushion to add a splash of colour or soften the sleek lines of the modern furniture.

Ian, dressed in a dark suit, hardly said a word as Chrissy, dressed in fawn chinos and a mint-green cashmere sweater was unable to keep quiet or still. She babbled away about the weather, local politics and the environment. Anything, except acknowledge why she was leading police officers through her home.

They ended up in an open-plan living room area, where Ian initially took a seat in the far corner. Fiona beckoned him to join them in the cluster of chairs facing the flat-screen television hung on the wall. Humphries sat beside Fiona while Rachel took the seat next to Chrissy.

When Fiona asked Chrissy to go through the morning's events up to when her daughter Skye was taken, she collapsed into tears, unable to speak, leaving her husband to provide scant details in a monotone. After retelling his wife's version of events, Ian silently stared at his feet.

Chrissy jumped from her chair. "Sorry, you said you wanted to talk in the garden."

Before anyone could stop her, they found themselves marched back through the warren of rooms. They walked through the courtyard and mature gardens to a picnic bench overlooking a fenced-off river. The Cotswold stone façade that lined the bustling thoroughfare gave no indication of the size of the outbuildings and gardens hidden behind the house.

"Is here, okay?" Chrissy asked nervously. "There's a bridge farther along to the other side. We fenced off this section of the river when Skye was born to prevent any accidents,"

"Here is perfect," Fiona quickly said, indicating they should sit.

In a daze, the Bonds awkwardly arranged their long limbs on one side of the bench. Chrissy checked the reception on her phone before placing it on the table in front of her. Once everyone was settled, Chrissy insisted Fiona and Humphries should have been offered refreshments and repeatedly apologised for her oversight. Fiona did her best to reassure Chrissy they didn't need a drink but fearing she was about to descend into another bout of tears, it was agreed Rachel should return to the house to make them all a drink.

Watching Rachel leave, Chrissy said, "Things like this happen to other people. Not people like us. We're respectful people. We socialise with our friends, here mostly, and don't bother anyone else." Looking up, she asked, "Why has this happened to us? We've never harmed or upset anyone. We regularly host charity events and do all we can to support local businesses and schools."

Fiona pushed an annoying strand of hair behind her ear, preparing herself for the reply.

"Unless …," Ian looked up at his wife before continuing. "Chrissy thinks I'm being silly, but I've been following the cases of two other girls who were abducted because they looked so similar to our Skye. The newspaper said you were arresting a German. Is this some bizarre, far-right, Aryan-race thing?"

"No, absolutely not. The press is speculating and getting it wrong," Fiona said sternly. She decided to risk asking Chrissy, who seemed more composed than earlier, if she would mind giving her version of what had happened that morning.

"I'm sorry. I can't tell you anything more than what my husband said. It all happened so quickly. The motorbike came from nowhere, and by the time I had come to my senses, it was gone."

"Have you seen or heard a motorcycle hanging around the area recently? Or maybe just an engine starting up?" Humphries asked.

"No, nothing out of the ordinary. The windows are double glazed, so we don't hear any noises from the street outside," Chrissy replied.

"How about you, Ian?"

"Nothing springs to mind."

"Have either of you sensed you were being watched or has anyone shown a special interest in Skye recently?" As Chrissy and Ian shook their heads, Fiona added, "It could be something as tiny as a stranger smiling as they passed or commenting on the weather?"

"Nothing out of the ordinary," Chrissy finally said. "Skye is such a bonny child that everyone loves her."

Fiona made a mental note to come back to the issue later. Lowering her voice, she asked as gently as she could, "Was Skye conceived naturally?"

"Of course, she was. What sort of question is that?" Ian snapped.

"Please, this is important," Fiona said, noticing Chrissy shift awkwardly in her seat. "Was Skye conceived naturally?"

"Ian replied, "Yes," again, but with less conviction.

"We can't help you unless you are honest with us." After a pause, Fiona asked, "Did you meet Dr Jeffrey when you were trying to conceive?"

Ian started to deny any knowledge, but Chrissy spoke over him. "Will telling you help to get Skye back?"

"Possibly."

"Ian is trying to protect me. We had accepted we would remain childless when Dr Jeffrey was recommended to me by a friend. It was all very clinical. Once I felt her growing inside me, I blanked out that she wasn't really mine. Family and friends were surprised at the pregnancy so late in life. I felt some of them disapproved, so we decided the keep the truth to ourselves."

Rachel appeared with a tray of coffees. She handed them out before sliding onto the bench next to Chrissy.

"Are you still in contact with the friend who introduced you?" Fiona asked.

"I haven't seen or heard from her recently, but I should have her number somewhere." Chrissy reached for her phone. Despite it being face-up on the table throughout their conversation, she checked for any new messages before scrolling through her contacts. She turned the phone to face Fiona. "Susan Penrose. That's her number there."

Fiona was sure it was the same number they had been given earlier by Melanie but jotted it down anyway. "How did you know Susan?"

"Before having Skye, I crammed my days with all manner of things. After work, there were yoga classes, theatre and wine appreciation groups, art classes. Oh, all sorts. Most of the groups used Berth university facilities. I think I met her at yoga, but I could be wrong. It could have been some other class. We hit it off right away."

"When did you last see her?"

"Maybe five years ago. My life changed when Skye arrived. I couldn't keep up with everything."

Placing her mug on one side, Fiona said, "Do you remember the name of the clinic you used?"

"We saw Dr Jeffrey, privately," Chrissy said, before looking away and dabbing her eyes with a tissue.

Ian defensively took over the explanation. "We visited Dr Jeffrey in a flat in Berth. She was highly recommended by my wife's friend, and that was good enough for me. We were ready to start a family. We didn't want to wait for years only to find NHS funding and policy had changed, and we no longer met their requirements. The constant questions from well-meaning friends and family were wearing my … us down. Dr Jeffrey's set-up suited us perfectly. Everything about the way she worked relaxed and put us at ease."

Fiona looked across at Chrissy, who had detached herself from the conversation. Her face was downcast hiding her expression, but every so often, her shoulders would shrug in time with a sob.

"What has any of this got to do with finding our Skye?" Ian asked. "She's out there alone, and you're asking us these completely irrelevant questions."

"We have reasons to believe your answers will help us to discover who took your daughter. I know it's difficult, but please could you try to answer my questions. I only have a few more." When Ian nodded his acceptance, Fiona asked, "Could you confirm the address Dr Jeffrey used?"

"It was so long ago I couldn't tell you. It was a turning off the main Landsdown Road. That's all I can remember. Before you ask, we paid Dr Jeffrey personally, in cash."

"When you visited Dr Jeffrey, did you see other people? A receptionist or other couples, perhaps?"

"No, it was decorated as a private house," Ian replied. "We only saw the small examination room, but I understand there was also a lab on that floor. We weren't interested in all that. We just wanted a baby."

"Did you have any say in picking the donors?"

"Well, yes. It was the main appeal of the programme. If we couldn't use our own genes, we wanted to make the best choice possible. We selected the donors on the basis of their academic history."

"Were you aware of their physical appearance?" Fiona asked.

"We were, but that didn't affect our judgement."

"If I showed you a series of photographs, would you be able to recognise your donors?"

"Maybe. Possibly. I remember he was tall and blond, but it was a long time ago." After staring intently at the pictures, Fiona handed to him, Ian said, "Does one of these men have our Skye? If he has harmed her in any way, I'll kill him."

"Do you recognise any of them?"

Ian shook his head and muttered, "It was years ago."

"Chrissy?"

Rachel took the series of pictures from Fiona and started to look through them with Chrissy. After studying them, Chrissy pointed to Carston and said, "Him, possibly. But I can't be sure."

"Can you describe the female donor?" Fiona asked, as she started to pull the series of photographs including Elaine Black from her folder.

"She was a university student. I remember that," Ian said. "Also, blonde. Curly, I think."

Chrissy stared at the photographs before pointing to Elaine Black and glaring at her husband. "You said at the time how attractive she was. You joked if you weren't with me, you might try to find her." She jumped from her seat and started to slap his face. "Is that what you did? Have you given her our baby girl? Have you?"

Ian shook his head but made no attempt to defend himself from his wife's slaps. Finally, she broke down in tears, and he wrapped his arms around her. "Don't be silly. You know I would never look at anyone else."

Chrissy pushed him away. She screamed, "Liar! I don't know anything anymore. I don't know you," before rushing from the garden toward the house. Rachel gave a shrug before following her.

CHAPTER FORTY-ONE

Back in the car, Humphries said, "Well, that went well."

"It was always going to be difficult for them, but it confirmed what we already suspected. We need to focus on how we are going to find this woman."

"Do you think there's any truth in Chrissy saying her husband may have tried to contact the woman?"

"I'll let things settle down and then ring Rachel," Fiona said. "She'll be better placed to try to find out. After updating Peter, let's see if we can find this guy who provides dodgy plates."

◆ ◆ ◆

After speaking to a few residents, Fiona and Humphries found Nobby with his head under the bonnet of an ancient Land Rover that looked like it should have been taken off the road a decade ago. He straightened up and gave them a goofy smile as he wiped his oily hands on an equally oily rag he pulled from his overalls. "Can I help you?"

"Hopefully," Fiona said, while Humphries circled the vehicle peering in the windows.

Distracted by Humphries, the smile slipped as recognition that they were police officers filled his eyes. "I've done nothing wrong. I'm just helping a mate out by looking at his car."

Humphries started to count the other vehicles littering the area. "Popular guy. You must have a lot of mates."

"I guess I have," Nobby replied. "That's not a crime, is it?"

"We're not interested in what you're doing for these mates

of yours. Unless one of them happened to be your old school-teacher, Elaine Black."

"Teach? I haven't seen her since I left that dump. So no, she's not on my list of mates."

"Are you sure about that?" Humphries asked. "I understand she was very popular with her students. A bit like you are. She didn't pop by to see how your career was taking off? Maybe ask you to look at her spark plugs?"

"Get out of here. Nothing like that went on."

"Like what?"

Growing impatient, Fiona said, "I don't want to take you down to the station away from your work, but we do need to know if you helped Elaine out with a vehicle recently. A motorcycle. What was it, again?"

"A Royal Enfield Interceptor," Humphries said.

"Not a bad bike if you like that type of thing, but I'm not a fan," Nobby said. "I don't work on bikes, anyway. Just cars."

"How about number plates?"

"Yeah, every vehicle needs a number plate. It's the law, don't you know."

"Stop jerking us about," Humphries said. "Did you provide Elaine with a motorcycle and false number plates?"

"Absolutely not."

"So, if I went rummaging about the back there," Humphries, said nodding towards the lock-up behind them, "I wouldn't find anything. No invoices, cash or old plates?"

"You can't go looking around people's stuff for no reason. I know my rights. You need a warrant or something official-like."

"Unless there's probable cause," Humphries said. "What do you think?" he asked Fiona. "Do you think there's probable cause, here?"

Leaving Nobby looking confused and anxious for her reply, Fiona walked away to answer her phone. She returned a few moments later to say, "No probable cause today." Looking at Humphries, she said, "We've got to go." Once in the car, she said, "We've got a possible address for Elaine. It's only a few miles from here. Peter wants us to interview the farmer who has rented his cottage to Ellie Gibson while he organises a possible backup team."

CHAPTER FORTY-TWO

Susan's body was covered with sweat as she writhed through every contraction. As each contraction eased, her wrists burned where she had strained against the handcuffs, which were now tightly chained to the bed's headrest. Through gritted teeth, she begged, "More pain killers, please."

From the bottom of the bed, Elaine said, "You don't need any more. You're doing fine. Breathe like I told you. It will all be over soon."

They breathed together until Susan braced herself against another surge of pain. As it subsided, she asked, "And then what?"

"I'll have my family."

"And what about me?"

"You? You can go to hell." As Susan suffered another surge of pain, Elaine moved to the top of the bed and slapped her. "Don't push, I said. Not yet. Wait until I tell you."

CHAPTER FORTY-THREE

Fiona and Humphries drove past Willow Cottage on their way to the farmhouse. Fiona pulled in further along the lane. Twisting to look back through the rear windows, she said, "The cottage is set well back from the road. Plenty of cover from the bushes. It can hardly be seen from the gate."

"It looked more like an old stone barn, surrounded by fields of barley than a house," Humphries said. "The driveway is a narrow strip of hardcore. In winter, it's probably only accessible with a tractor or a four-by-four. A perfect spot for someone wanting to hide."

Fiona restarted the car and pulled away from the grass verge. "We best get on to speak to this farmer to check it is Elaine in there. We won't be popular if she spots us and decides to make a quick getaway."

The main farm entrance was a short distance along the road. Like the cottage, it was set back a distance from the lane, behind a gate and high hedges. That's where the similarity ended. The smooth driveway was lined by paddocks of grazing horses. The driveway led them around the side of the house into a neat courtyard surrounded by old, stone stabling. A pathway ran from the stables to an impressive sand arena with a complete set of painted show jumps glistening in the sunshine.

Leaving their car, they were approached by a woman spinning the wheels of her wheelchair towards them. Fiona judged the woman to be in her late sixties, but physically healthy and robust despite the obvious disability. Dressed in a T-shirt, jeans and jodhpur boots, she gave the impression she could leap from her chair onto one of the nearby horses at any moment.

"Hello, I'm Beth. I'm afraid my husband is away, so you will have to do with me."

"Oh. We were told he was waiting here for us to arrive," Fiona said.

"He was, but some fool has left the gate open in the lower field, and our cattle are out." Banging her hands on the side of the wheelchair, Beth added, "My days of chasing after errant bullocks are long gone."

"Do you know how long he will be?"

"As long as it takes to herd them all back where they belong and padlock the damn gate. Bloody ramblers will have to climb over it in future. The fine weather always brings them out. Do you want to come in or talk over there in the shade?" Beth asked, pointing to a wooden bench to their right."

"Outside is fine." Taking a seat, Fiona asked, "We are here about your tenant of Willow cottage. Have you met her?"

"No, my husband dealt with them. I saw them drive in with their truck. Since then, I've seen them speeding by on their motorbike numerous times. Good job, they come and go at odd hours when there's no other traffic about, or my husband would have had to pull them out of a hedge by now."

"Them? We understood the cottage was rented to a woman?" Fiona asked, already starting to have doubts they had found Elaine.

"She made the booking and paid the rent, but there's a bloke with her. To be honest, it would be a lonely old place for a town girl to stay by herself for six months."

"Six months?"

"She said that was how long her contract was for, and as she would be claiming the money back, she was happy to pay up-front."

"Do you know what the contract was or who it was with?" Fiona asked.

"Filming of some description, I think. Those TV dramas like using our quiet country lanes and isolated spots. People in the village say they can earn more money renting their house out to them for a few days than what they earn working for a year. Which company it is? I haven't a clue."

"Are you able to describe her from the glimpses you've had?" Fiona asked.

"I've only seen her from a distance or going by on the back of the motorcycle. Average height, slim with dark, spikey hair."

"And the man who is staying with her in the cottage?"

"Again, I've not actually met him. Black, tall and slim. They seem quite young. Mid-twenties, I would guess."

Fiona went through the motions of pulling up the picture they had of Elaine Black. As it was a close-up of an attractive blonde woman, she guessed it was a waste of time. "Could this be the woman renting the cottage?"

Beth screwed her eyes up as she closely examined the picture. "Even with the right colour hair, I couldn't say one way or the other. Could it be forwarded onto my husband?"

Her husband called back within minutes to say he couldn't commit himself to anything more definite than, possibly and that he would be busy for a while.

Fiona asked Beth, "Is there any other way in and out of the cottage other than the driveway?"

"The cottage used to be the old dairy. The drive is part of a track that runs across most of our land. It comes out on mill lane just below the village." After showing Fiona the track on Google Map, Beth said, "Could I take another look at that photograph?"

"Sure," Fiona said, handing over the image.

Beth chewed her lip as she scrutinised the picture. She stared into the distance, looking increasingly frustrated. Returning the photograph, she said, "Sorry. I thought for a minute I did recognise her, but I can't say for sure. I can't remember where I might have seen her other than I don't think she is our tenant." Shaking her head in frustration, she added, "I generally never forget a face, and she seems familiar, somehow."

"Are you thinking you met her recently?" Fiona asked.

"Yes. In the last few weeks, but I can't place where for the life of me."

"Think about where you have been the last few weeks. That might help," Fiona suggested.

Beth gave a hollow laugh. "Before the stupid accident, I would have been here, there and everywhere, either socialising, working on the farm or preparing horses for sale. Now, I rarely go anywhere except the supermarket, the pharmacy or the local hospital." Her face lit up with recognition. "That's it. The pharmacy in Tarkington. That's where I saw her. It would have been at the start of the month. That's when I always pick up my medication."

"Are you sure it was the start of this month?"

Beth thought for a while. "I am absolutely sure it was this month. I was in the queue behind her. I didn't recognise her as being from being around here, but she seemed friendly enough. She was babbling away about her daughter being ill. I'm afraid I wasn't taking that much notice of her or what she was saying."

CHAPTER FORTY-FOUR

Fiona updated Peter, and they drove back toward Willow Cottage.

"You don't think it's her in the cottage, then?" Humphries asked.

"You heard what I said to Peter. No, nothing fits. According to her husband and work colleagues, she was a quiet, unassuming teacher assistant who rarely socialised prior to her disappearance. Where could she have linked up with this man prepared to go along with her crazy plan? We would look stupid storming the place with a full team."

"We will look even more stupid if it is her, and we allow her to escape."

"It's not her," Fiona replied firmly. "They are leaving the cottage unoccupied for hours on end, every day. The girls aren't in there. It's a shame we don't have the name of the television company to check their story, but no, I don't think this is the right Ellie Gibson."

"I'm just playing the Devil's Advocate, so hear me out," Humphries said. "The time she arrived and paying cash upfront for six months ties in with everything else."

"We've never once considered she was working with someone else. Her husband gave the impression their marriage was solid before the depression hit. From everything we know about her, this feels wrong." Fiona said, parking the car in the same spot as before, just past the entrance to Willow Cottage. "Peter is sending someone out to the pharmacy. That is the best lead we've got. Hopefully, we've still got a bit of time to track her down. Susan is heavily pregnant, and I don't think Elaine plans on moving on to start her new life until that child is born."

"How do we know Susan hasn't given birth already?"

"We don't, but on her track record, I think once Elaine has taken safe delivery of the baby, she'll have no qualms killing Susan, and we haven't found a body, yet."

"She could be lying dead in there as we speak," Humphries said, nodding toward the cottage. "We could be wasting time here while Elaine is long gone with another new identity we don't know about."

"Are you arguing for the sake of it, or do you think it's her in there?"

"I don't like the idea of us sitting here twiddling our thumbs if she is in there with those girls. I know we haven't considered the possibility she was working with someone else, but maybe she is. It would explain a few things."

"Such as?"

"Everyone we spoke to described Elaine as kind and thoughtful," Humphries said. "She goes out of her way to help others, especially her students. What if she's only interested in taking the children, and it's him who has been doing the killing?"

"I hear what you're saying but working with someone else suggests an element of pre-planning. The evidence indicates that the GP telling her she couldn't have children was the sudden catalyst for her to set out to retrieve what in her muddled mind she considers to be her daughters."

"Grabbing the children, yes. But the stabbing of Dr Jeffrey and Emily? What if that was him?"

After a short consideration, Fiona said, "The cameras at the clinic caught someone slight, probably female. And Melanie's neighbour described the intruder as slight."

"Nobody was attacked on either of those occasions. There is no footage of who left the murder scenes."

Before Fiona could respond, Peter called to say a patrol car was blocking the track behind the cottage, and they were primed to assist if required. Ending the call, Fiona turned the car around and parked it in front of the gate. "Come on, then," she said, opening the car door. "I thought you were the one keen to get in there."

"We're walking up the drive?"

"Yes, come on," Fiona said, opening the boot of the car. "Sorry," she said, handing over a vest. "Peter insisted if we are going in alone."

"What's our pretext for knocking on the door?"

"Two fugitives were seen heading this way before disappearing off the radar. We're checking she is okay and whether she has seen anything."

Fiona was as reluctant as Humphries to put on the uncomfortable vests. As they drew closer, the cottage looked neglected and empty. The lawn and shrubs lining the drive were overgrown, and dandelions grew in tufts around the front door. The image Humphries created of Susan lying dead inside on the floor refused to leave her mind as they took the final few steps up to the front door. What if she was wrong and Elaine was in there?

Humphries pressed the doorbell and banged the door knocker several times before lifting the letterbox flap and calling out, "Hello." Fiona felt the first trickle of sweat run down her side. It became an irritating itch she couldn't scratch under the unyielding vest as the silence dragged on. Humphries stepped back and looked up at the upper windows before saying, "Shall I go and get the crowbar?"

"Don't you want to try the back door, first?" Fiona asked.

Moving to the side to peer into a window, Humphries replied, "Somebody is staying here. There are a couple of mugs on the table and what looks like a jacket on the floor." Straightening, he added, "The back door will probably be easier to force, anyway."

CHAPTER FORTY-FIVE

Fiona wandered back to the front of the house while Humphries collected the crowbar from the car. Even though she thought his theory of two people working together was unlikely, the possibility played on her mind as she scanned the surrounding area. It was a perfect location if someone wanted to stay hidden. She shuddered at the thought of Susan's mangled body lying on the other side of the door. She turned at the sound of shouting as two irritable looking people marched down the drive with Humphries.

"What the hell is going on here? How dare you block our entrance."

Fiona was relieved they hadn't made a start on breaking down the back door. The painfully thin, pale woman approaching was most definitely not Elaine Black. She looked nothing like her, was at least ten years younger and had a London accent. As the couple squared up to her, she could see the television production company lanyards hanging around their necks. She stepped to one side and said, "Humphries. Can you handle this while I update Peter?"

"Thanks," Humphries muttered. "You give me all the best jobs."

Fiona had to walk a fair distance away to make her call over the sound of shouting. The volume had reduced slightly by the time she walked over to join the furore. The man looked like he was finding the situation amusing, but the woman was still in raging-bull mode. Her face was flushed with anger as she turned on Fiona.

"You're the person in charge of this circus, I understand."

"Yes, I apologise for the shock you've received. Has my colleague explained we received information that suggested three little girls may have been held hostage inside?"

Daggers flew from the woman's eyes. First directed toward Fiona and then Humphries. She pointed at Humphries and said, "He said there was a dangerous fugitive on the loose, and you feared for our safety."

Realising Humphries had used her planned excuse for visiting the property had they been in, Fiona quickly said, "Yes. A fugitive who has snatched three children. Clearly, the information we received was incorrect. I can only apologise for disturbing you. With children involved, we acted as soon as the information came in. Their safe return is our number one priority."

The red of the woman's face started to recede, revealing a splattering of freckles over almost porcelain, white skin. "I understand you are doing your job, but it concerns me how our right to privacy has been railroaded on someone else's word." She turned full circle, looking uncomfortable. "Hang on. This isn't one of those candid camera things, is it? Have we been set up as some kind of practical joke? I bet it was Jimmy. This is the sort of stupid stunt he would pull for a laugh."

"No, it really isn't," Fiona said, although she was pleased to note the thought that this was a filmed prank had re-directed the woman's fury. Maybe she now regretted the explosive expletives she had been firing at Humphries while Fiona spoke to Peter.

"Who made the phone call tipping you off? If it wasn't a joke, it could have been one of our competitors hoping to trash our reputation and get us tied up in paperwork."

Reading the name on the woman's lanyard, Fiona said, "The person we are looking for is using your name, although I doubt it is anything personal. Just a chance thing." Any connection was unlikely, but she asked, anyway, "Did you go to Berth University?"

The woman laughed. "Local Tech college and far too many free gigs was my only training."

Humphries said, "Should we check inside before we leave? Just in case? For your safety."

The man pulled the house door key from his pocket. Dangling it off a forefinger, he said, "We've nothing to hide. You're welcome to verify there is no one else here."

After a cursory look around the cottage, Fiona handed over her card, and said, "Thank you for your time and understanding."

"Just find those little girls and we might forget about it."

CHAPTER FORTY-SIX

Overtaking the disappointment about Willow Cottage was an air of nervous expectation in the incident room. The paperwork demanding the pharmacy release the address being used by Ellie Gibson had been initiated, but everyone was hoping Abbie and Steve could obtain the address voluntarily.

Not seeing Peter in the room, Fiona headed over to knock on his office door. He looked tired and out of place behind the mound of paperwork, but his face broke into a wide smile when he saw her and invited her to sit. "Sorry about the mess up at Willow Cottage. It has now been confirmed that the Ellie Gibson you met today is who she claims to be. Are they going to make a complaint?"

"I think we managed to smooth things over. I'm just as much to blame. I should have insisted on speaking to the farmer who rented the cottage rather than relying on his wife, who admitted she hadn't met their tenants. Even if it was going to involve wading through a sea of muck behind a load of cows. It didn't sit right with me as soon as I heard there was a man with her. I should have trusted my instincts and done a more thorough check. At least we didn't go in there with a full backup team."

"True, but we should have checked this end before sending you out there."

"But then we wouldn't have had the possible sighting at the pharmacist. It makes sense. She would need something to keep the girls quiet and manageable while she waits for Susan to give birth."

"You're convinced that's what she's waiting for?"

"That's what my gut is telling is me," Fiona replied.

"I think you're right," Peter said. "Sorry, if I was a bit sharp this morning. I'm frustrated with this case, but I shouldn't have taken it out on everyone else."

"Are you feeling okay?" Fiona joked, realising this was the first time she had ever heard Peter fully apologise for anything. She quickly added, "I should have spoken to the pupils the first time around. We would have had the alias Elaine is using far sooner."

"We're all fallible," Peter replied.

Fiona gave him a hard look before saying, "Are you sure everything is okay?"

"Tired and fed up, but I'm fine. Changing the subject, have you managed to persuade the other witness who saw Eliot McCall the night the girl was strangled to speak to you?"

Fiona shook her head. "No, he has made it clear he doesn't want to help us. I could call the station with an anonymous tip-off about Eliot. While his father made sure nothing was officially recorded if they dug around, they would discover he was questioned for a similar attack."

"Don't do that. Leave it with me," Peter said, before reaching across to answer his phone. As he listened, he gave Fiona the thumbs up and started tapping on his laptop. Ending the call, he swung the laptop screen around to face Fiona. "The pharmacist has given us a name and an address." Pointing to the screen, he continued, "He confirmed she is going by the name Ellie, and this is the temporary address she gave. The only access by car is down this dead-end lane, but there are possible routes out through the woods behind the property on foot or on a motorcycle. We have a positive, physical identification this time. Can I leave setting everything up to you?"

"On it," Fiona said, rising from her seat.

"Check ownership of the cottage, and if everything is looking good, take a full team with you this time. Abbie and Steve are driving straight to the address to watch the front entrance. Officers will have to make their way on foot to cover the rear access. There's nothing to suggest she is armed, but we know she's handy with a knife, so I want everyone in vests. Oh, and as we think the girls are in there, contact the child protection unit in Birstall for an experienced officer to attend."

Fiona edged toward the door, keen to update the team and get the ball rolling. "I know the drill."

"Yes, sorry. I know you do. Once everything is in place, call me, and I'll join you out there."

Fiona shot out the door and jogged along the corridor to the incident room. A sea of expectant eyes met her. Unable to prevent a satisfied smile from spreading across her face, she said, "Steve and Abbie did good. We have an address."

A collective, "Yes!" punctured the air.

Pulling up the address on her computer screen, Fiona asked Rachel to contact the owner of the cottage and Humphries to contact the Birstall child protection unit. She organised a team, drafting in as many officers as she could get hold of at short notice. She explained the positions she wanted them to take up while they waited for Rachel and Humphries to report back.

CHAPTER FORTY-SEVEN

The adrenaline was pumping by the time Fiona led the small team to the entrance of Manor Cottage. Unlike outside Willow Cottage, she was convinced Elaine, the girls and Susan Penrose were inside the building. Short though the driveway was, there was a lot that could go wrong between where she was standing at the entrance and releasing everyone unharmed. She took a deep breath when the final confirmation that everyone was in place came through. "Ready?"

"I guess," Humphries replied. "Nervous?"

"A bit. You?"

"I just want this over and done with."

Peter appeared to wish them luck before they started their walk along the driveway to the house. "You're absolutely sure on the plan?"

Fiona and Humphries nodded. "We will see you inside in ten minutes, all being well."

"And we will make last orders in a pub," Steve called after them.

Walking down the drive, an upstairs light went on. "We know someone's in," Humphries said.

"Not necessarily. It could be on a timer," Fiona replied.

At the front door, Humphries said, "Relax. It's going to go like clockwork," before he rang the doorbell.

They could hear the bell ringing inside but there was no sound of any response. He rang it again, keeping his finger pressed down on the buzzer. Humphries released the buzzer, and they exchanged looks before Fiona called through the letter slot, "Ellie? Are you in there?"

Humphries returned his finger to the buzzer.

Fiona knocked his hand away. "Shh! What was that? I thought I heard a child's voice," she said, pressing her ear to the door. Hearing nothing more, she turned to shout through the letter slot. "Hello? Are you in there?" She straightened up. "I can't hear anything more, but I'm sure I heard something."

Humphries took her place, lifted the letterbox flap and shouted, "Could you open the door, Ellie?"

Fiona walked away and beckoned one of the uniformed officers waiting at the side of the houses over. "We're not getting any response."

A uniformed officer set to work on the door. Moments later, he threw his weight against the door, pushing it wide open. Fiona and Humphries followed him and his colleague in, with Steve and Abbie behind them. As the uniformed officers started checking the downstairs, Fiona and Humphries headed upstairs. Fiona turned right at the top of the stairs, and Humphries went left, checking each room as they went. She was opening the final door when she heard Humphries shout.

"Over here! I think I've found the girls."

Fiona dashed back along the corridor. She could now hear high-pitched screaming. Humphries knelt by the keyhole to the locked door, pleading with the girls to calm down and move away from the door so they could break in. She put her hand on his back and indicated he could step back so she could try to reason with them.

Kneeling by the door, she said, "Hi, my name is Fiona. I'm a police officer here to rescue you and take you back to your parents." Her initial attempts at calming the girls seemed to make matters worse. Some people were naturals around children. She wasn't one of them. Whenever friends insisted that she hold their babies within seconds of being in her arms, the little bundles of joy stiffened and started to cry. She looked helplessly around at Humphries, who shrugged in return. She tried again to calm the girls through the keyhole, and slowly the screaming subsided. She thought it was more due to exhaustion than her soothing effect, as she reassured them that she was one of the good guys come to rescue them.

Over quiet sobbing, one child said, "That's what she said."

"Hi, is that Katie? Or Amber or Skye?" Receiving no reply, Fiona said, "I need you all to move back away from the door, so we can break it down. Can you do that?" As Humphries approached the door with a crowbar, she heard the muffled sound of movement and what sounded like the clinking of chains. Once Humphries started on the door, it gave little resistance. Fiona took a deep breath to ready herself to enter the room.

Inside were three single beds with matching My Little Pony duvet sets. Three blonde girls in pink, My Little Princess nighties huddled together on the middle bed. Three sets of wide blue eyes stared at her, not quite daring to hope their ordeal was over. As she slowly approached the bed, the three girls hugged each other tightly.

From behind her, Humphries said, "I'll get the bolt cutters up here."

Over her shoulder, Fiona said, "As soon as the house has the all-clear, get the child expert up here."

The oldest looking girl asked, "Are you really the police?"

Fiona smiled and handed over her warrant card. "I am. And you must be Skye. We'll get those chains off you and get you out of here. Your families are desperate to see you."

"Is my mommy still dead?" Katie asked.

"I'm afraid so," Fiona said, a lump forming in her throat as the innocent, hopeful look in Katie's eye faded away.

"What about *her*?" the child in the middle of the huddle asked. "She said that she was our mother, now."

"You must be Amber," Fiona said, slightly disorientated by how similar the three girls looked. "You don't have to worry about her anymore."

Humphries re-entered the room carrying the bolt cutters as Fiona did her best to reassure the wide-eyed girls that removing the cuffs wasn't going to hurt a bit.

As the chains were cut, Fiona stepped back and whispered to Humphries, "Have they found Elaine and Susan?"

Steve appeared in the doorway, and said, "Come with me." As he led her out of the room, he explained they had discovered a locked door to a cellar. It was proving harder to get through, but they hoped to have it open shortly. They were halfway down the main staircase when they heard the screech of metal and wood splintering, followed by boots charging down a series of steps.

Fiona started to rush down the remaining steps, but Steve grabbed her arm. Over the commotion going on beneath them, he said, "We'll wait at the foot of the stairs as the last line of defence in case she manages to get past them."

Fiona agreed as there were more than enough officers to overpower one woman. She turned towards the cellar as the sound of a scuffle broke out. Over the shouts, a woman was screaming, "My baby. My baby. I'm not leaving without her. She needs me."

Leaning against the bannisters, Steve said, "I guess they've found Elaine. A good result all around. I'm looking forward to seeing DCI Hillier's reaction when he discovers he was utterly wrong about Amber's abduction."

"Is that all you care about?" Fiona asked. "Those poor girls have been chained to beds by a madwoman. God only knows what she has been saying to them."

"At least they had each other. That must have helped."

"There is that, I suppose," Fiona replied.

"So, where do you guys go for a celebratory drink around here?"

"By the time we've processed everything, the pubs will be shut. The team might go somewhere to celebrate the result tomorrow."

"You're kidding, right? There must be somewhere that stays open late." Reading Fiona's expression correctly, Steve said, "I forgot we're out in the sticks here. Well, you will just have to go into Birstall for the evening."

"Maybe," Fiona said. "I will wait to see what the others want to do."

"You won't come without them? Not even if I ask very nicely?"

Fiona avoided replying by diverting Steve's attention to the procession moving along the hallway. Officers were half-carrying a red-faced Elaine from the cellar. She managed to twist and turn in their grasp, screaming for her baby, despite her hands being firmly cuffed behind her back. Spotting Fiona and Steve on the staircase, she tried to lunge towards them. "You had better not have touched my girls! If you have, you will rot in hell!"

Fiona dropped her gaze to the floor to avoid antagonising the situation. It was hard to reconcile the writhing woman with her face distorted by anger and hatred with an unassuming, caring teacher. In her current state, a lawyer would easily argue she was unfit for questioning and possibly trial. Academic in many ways as Elaine was going to serve a long sentence whether it was in prison or a mental health facility.

Fiona was relieved they had found the girls physically unharmed, but it didn't feel like a victory. Mostly she felt sad with no inclination to join the others in a celebration. Two, possibly three women were dead, and Elaine was seriously disturbed. It was hard for her to not have some sympathy despite all she had done.

CHAPTER FORTY-EIGHT

Fiona's stomach lurched when she saw Eddie looking pale and shaken, emerge from the cellar. He had been around long enough to not be distressed by murder scenes and veered towards the same coping mechanism of gallows humour as Humphries. Whatever Elaine had done to Susan, it wasn't pretty. After watching Eddie head out the front door, presumably in need of fresh air, she turned towards the cellar door.

Steve caught Fiona's arm and said, "You don't have to," nodding toward the cellar door. "We all have enough horror in our memory banks to keep us awake at night without adding to it unnecessarily. By my reckoning, there are plenty of other officers down there."

The officer who forced the front door appeared in the hallway, followed by Andrew. "Ah, Fiona. Peter wants you down there straight away. We're all apparently useless." Laughing, Andrew added, "Go on, then. It's not that bad."

Andrew blocked Steve from going along the narrow corridor with Fiona. "Not you. We've got other stuff to do."

With an anxious look back at Steve, Fiona prepared herself to remain calm whatever she found at the bottom of the stairs. The steps were steep without lighting or a handrail. As she carefully made her way down, she heard a scream that went straight through her, followed by a string of swear words. She pushed open the small wooden door as Susan screamed, "I'm going to die."

"No, you're not," Peter calmly said in response, although Fiona could see him grimace as Susan crushed his hand in hers. As Susan released her grip, Peter flexed his fingers and quietly said, "Now, breathe with me until it's time to push again." Looking up at Fiona, he said, "Get the other end. Have you delivered a baby before?"

Uncertain where to look or what to do, and not sure whether to laugh or cry, Fiona replied, "Funny enough, no. Have you?"

"I watched all my children being born," Peter replied.

Before Fiona could respond, Susan started shouting, "Oh! Oh! Oh!"

"Okay. Look at me," Peter said to Susan. "We're nearly there. One more big push."

Fiona moved to the end of the bed, feeling petrified. "What do I do?"

Peter was too busy encouraging Susan to take any notice of her. Accepting she would have to make it up as she went, Fiona picked up a folded towel and looked on helplessly as Susan pushed again. Looking down, she said, "Oh my God. It's coming."

"I know!" Susan screamed, before almost levitating off the bed with the pain of another contraction.

"Okay, breathe with me," Peter said. Once Susan's attention was concentrated on him, he asked Fiona, "What can you see?"

"The top of a head, I think."

"Okay. One more big push and it will all be over." As Susan's face was contorted in pain, he continued to instruct her. "Now push."

Fiona forgot about her apprehension as the baby's head, followed by its shoulders, appeared. Instinctively, she reached down and eased the baby's arrival into the world.

"Well done, Susan," Peter said. "I knew you could do it."

Fiona carefully started to dry the baby before grabbing a clean towel and using it to tightly wrap the tiny body. She had just finished when the baby's face screwed up and started to howl. "Now, what do I do?"

"There are two clamps on the table behind you. Clamp them onto the umbilical cord and then cut it between them."

Still holding the baby against her chest with one arm, Fiona did as Peter instructed with her other shaky hand. She jumped back, thinking she had done something wrong when Susan experienced another contraction.

"Am I having twins?" Susan asked in a frightened voice.

"No, it's normal," Peter reassured her. "Bring the baby over, Fiona."

Fiona carefully placed the baby in Susan's waiting arms. She looked exhausted, her face flushed, and her hair matted, but the loving smile she gave her baby was the most beautiful thing Fiona had ever seen. The door behind banged open, and a pair of paramedics rushed into the room.

"A bit late," Peter said. "We've done all the hard work."

Before the paramedics pushed him out of the way, Susan grabbed Peter's hand again. "Thank you so much."

CHAPTER FORTY-NINE

Fiona pushed open the door to the Squire Inn. She found it hard to suppress a smile when she was greeted with a roar of approval and shouts of, "All hail the midwife," and "Call the midwife." By the looks of things, they had been hitting the beer hard for a while.

Steve shouted over the chatter, "What do you want?"

"An orange juice, please."

"Absolutely not," Humphries said. "She'll have a double gin and tonic. I will make sure she gets home safely."

"Just the one," Fiona conceded. "Make it a single," she added, as she dodged her way through the back-slapping and general high spirits to the bar.

Handing over her drink, Steve asked, "Where did you go after the briefing? I missed you."

They turned to chants of, "Down in one," as Humphries poured a pint down his throat. Slamming the empty glass on the bar, he said, "Shots, everyone," to cheers of agreement.

"Are you two joining us?"

Steve nodded, while Fiona quickly declined. After watching them down shots in synch, she caught sight of Peter stood at the end of the bar with a tankard of beer. He raised it in greeting, and she made her way over to him.

"How did it go at the hospital?"

"Okay," Fiona replied. "Susan is very up and down as she comes to terms with losing Emily and Katie and becoming a mother. I think she will prevail despite all she has been through. She's a strong person, and she's surrounded by friends."

"You can be lonely in a crowd," Peter said, before taking a drink of his beer.

"True. She told me a little more about the clinic and Dr Jeffrey. Because of Elaine's looks and intelligence, she was a popular choice of donor, and she was asked to donate far more regularly than medical standards allow. When Susan decided she wanted a child to complete their family, she contacted Dr Jeffrey because she thought it would be good for Katie to have a real sister."

"Family is more than blood," Peter said.

"I know. She had no idea that she had taken the last of the eggs that Elaine had provided. They had been frozen since Dr Jeffrey closed down her side enterprise. What do you think will happen to Elaine?"

"An insanity plea is looking likely." After taking a sip of beer, Peter added, "We caught her and returned the girls. That's the main thing."

"I guess. One good thing to come out of it all, is that the parents have agreed to the girls meeting up at regular intervals."

They turned as another cheer of encouragement came from their colleagues across the bar. Fiona caught Steve's eye. He gave her a quick smile before turning to join in whatever drinking game they were now involved in.

"Going to be some sore heads, tomorrow," Peter said. "You were grinning from ear to ear when you walked in. What was that all about?"

"You'll laugh at me."

"Me? Never." Looking across the pub, he asked, "Is there a thing going on between you and Steve?"

"No. Absolutely, not. He's not my type at all," Fiona said, sipping her drink. "If you must know, I held Susan's baby in the hospital. She has called her Emily, but ... her second name is Fiona." Patting Peter's shoulder, Fiona added, "It would have been Peter if it was a boy. You are still Susan's number one hero."

"Glad to hear it. What is happening with Katie? Is she still staying at Tasha's with Melanie?"

"For now," Fiona said. "Melanie took her to see her new sister this morning. Susan made it very clear she would be collecting Katie once she is released from hospital. She isn't going to give up custody without a fight."

"Good. I received a call before I left the station. There is going to be a full investigation into Dr Jeffrey's activities. It is doubted she was working alone. They will contact you for a statement."

"Okay. I assume they will start with the clinic. There is a consultant who moved with her from their parent company in London."

"I have some other news for you. I think you will like it." Rather than say what it was, Peter took a long drink from his pint, draining the glass. Placing it on the bar, he asked, "Same again? We can share a taxi."

"Go on, then." As soon as Peter ordered the drinks, Fiona asked, "This other news?"

Leaning over to whisper in her ear, Peter said, "Plymouth station have taken Eliot McCall in for questioning and are reviewing a previous case where he was interviewed"

"Yes," Fiona said, making a fist and giving a little thump into the air. "Now that I will drink to. Do you think they will investigate Dewhurst's role as the SIO?"

Peter shrugged. "You know someone like him will likely wriggle out of it and somehow end up with a promotion."

"As long as it's elsewhere, I don't really care," Fiona said.

"Shock, horror. I always thought you were driven by honour and integrity, not personal dislike."

"Normally, yes. But for him, I'll make an exception."

BOOKS IN THIS SERIES

A DI Fiona Williams Mystery

A Fiery End

Driving home late at night, DI Fiona Williams comes across a vehicle engulfed in flames. The driver is at the wheel, oblivious to the inferno surrounding him.

There is no explanation for why the vehicle was on the road or why the quiet tradesman was murdered in such a macabre way. The only witness to the fire, claims she saw nothing. Whatever she did see goes to the grave with her when she is brutally strangled. Frustration grows when the driver's daughter disappears.

With time running out to find the daughter alive, Fiona is drawn into a web of powerful men determined to keep their deadly games secret. Juggling a family crisis and a growing suspicion her boss is corrupt, her judgement is hampered by her attraction to the man central to everything.

BOOKS IN THIS SERIES

Fiona Williams Mystery

A Fiery End

Driving home late at night, DI Fiona Williams comes across a vehicle engulfed in flames. The driver is at the wheel, oblivious to the inferno surrounding him.There is no explanation for why the vehicle was on the road or why the quiet tradesman was murdered in such a macabre way. The only witness to the fire, claims she saw nothing. Whatever she did see goes to the grave with her when she is brutally strangled. Frustration grows when the driver's daughter disappears.With time running out to find the daughter alive, Fiona is drawn into a web of powerful men determined to keep their deadly games secret. Juggling a family crisis and a growing suspicion her boss is corrupt, her judgement is hampered by her attraction to the man central to everything.

A Mother's Ruin

A single mother is brutally murdered in her garden.

DI Fiona Williams interprets the crime scene differently from her colleagues but fears her history of failed relationships taints her judgment. The wrong decision will change the lives of three children forever.

In a male-dominated department, with mounting evidence

pointing in the other direction, will she find the courage to trust her instincts and narrow the investigation?

An intriguing mystery that blurs the distinction between the villain and the victim.

A Relative Death

An eye for an eye. A death for a death.
Some people will do anything for revenge.
And one detective will do anything to stop them.
DI Fiona Williams returns from a short break to a station stretched by the antics of a gang of youths, staff absences and three murders in quick succession. With unconnected victims and widely different murder methods, the only link is they seem motiveless. Forced to work in small groups rather than as a team, frustrations and jealousies flare-up between the officers creating a minefield of tension and a headache for Fiona.
As the most experienced officer, she is pulled from the initial case of a poisoned pensioner to investigate the shooting of a wealthy landowner's wife. She is annoyed the murder of a defenceless war veteran is given lower priority and thoughts of the pensioner's last moments are never far away.
The two victims have never met, and the only similarity is their murderer was someone who knew them well. The chances of it being the same person are remote.
When a breakthrough comes in the investigation, it seems Fiona's nagging thought that the cases are connected may be correct. To fit the missing pieces together she will have to risk her life for an enemy she has worked hard to condemn.

BOOKS BY THIS AUTHOR

The Skeletons Of Birkbury

One buried body.
Many hidden secrets.
When the body of a teenage girl is discovered, the villagers of Birkbury close ranks to protect their secrets.
Gossip turns to fear and suspicion as they realise the killer is one of them and is prepared to kill again.
Beneath the good manners and polite smiles, DCI Hatherall discovers deep-seated resentments and family feuds going back decades. The stakes are raised when another girl goes missing.
Will the police uncover the killer before it is too late?

Bells On Her Toes

Point Of No Return

Who Killed Vivien Morse?

Twisted Truth

The Paperboy

Trouble At Clenchers Mill

A Charming English village mystery
When a neighbour is accused of attempting to kill her ex-husband, Simon Morris jumps at the chance to practice his sleuthing skills and prove her innocence. His amateur investigations draw him into the murky world of village politics and on-line predators as he uncovers a collective effort to drive Richard Fielding and his new family out of Clenchers Mill. And behind the smokescreen of unpleasant bullying, there is one person who is determined to see Richard dead.
Without some quick thinking and the help of his dogs, Simon's first case may prove to be the death of them all.

Trouble At Fatting House

Trouble At Suncliffe Manor

Debts & Druids

Fool Me Once

A Fiery End

Printed in Great Britain
by Amazon